A FORK IN THE ROAD

A FORK IN THE ROAD

James W. Swanson

ReadersMagnet, LLC

CONTENTS

PART ONE

Heading East

S EVERAL PEOPLE BACK in Milbank thought I had a career in modeling. Maybe, but being attractive was a problem. For example, here in my new school, the upper class young men sought every opportunity to attract my attention. But even the most accomplished and handsome of the them discovered that I wasn't eager to choose one over the other or anyone at all. In fact, their interest annoyed me. I knew I commanded attention, as did several of the most popular young women, who I learned had formed a crew that excluded those who were neeky. I, on the other hand, although nicely dressed, neither paid much attention to the latest attire nor sought to be a member of their exclusive group. They, accordingly, had no desire to include me, seeing me as contrary and out of touch with popular expectations. Probably they roiled with the attention I received from the potential baes that they worked so hard to attract. Mostly I saw them standing in the hall in a huddle thumbing their phones like fingerless piano players. Don't get me wrong I spent more than enough time on my phone texting, buying stuff from Amazon with my parents permission which was never enough, but I understood, sort of. I wasn't stylin' with the scene girls or those who thought they were. I just liked nice things. Of course in our classes we couldn't use smart phones but our laptops and iPads were the links to our assignments and research, especially useful in biology, even in social studies, so I didn't discount the clique on their phones as much as the way they used them. And I had no wish to be a model.

When I think back about that time in my life I remember that the best thing that happened on my first day in Buford Post High School was Wendy, Wendy Westin, who sat beside me in biology class, not by accident, I discovered, but by her intent. She was an outgoing, attractive girl, who wanted to get acquainted with the newbie in school and to steer me in the right direction. I didn't think I needed steering but I liked her from the start. She admired Hayward Russell, our biology teacher who I had to admit was legit bumping for a teacher. We learned from our first day his passion about climate change. I hadn't really thought about that. In fact, I hadn't thought about much of anything except adjusting to my new environs, not that my old ones were so great back in Milbank, South Dakota except for Sherrie Miller, who I texted about everything that was going on.

The most sought after among the young men, Wendy told me, was the handsome senior quarterback of the football team who had, she said, a future with a division one university. He was that gnarly. He led the team to a record eighteen victories and two losses his junior and senior years. This young man noticed me from the start. I didn't doll myself up with cosmetics or frosting to attract attention. Now bear with me here: my naturally red lips, long eyelashes, soft, fair completion, and budding figure were enough to make the young men swoon and young women jealous. Ok, I admit it, I noticed him, certainly a masculine specimen to anyone who was interested. But I wasn't. He attempted to engage me in conversation with his pleasant grin that indicated he, like me, knew how stylin' he was without even trying. I ignored him except for a brief smile of acknowledgement. Whatever attention I paid him infuriated a few of the young women, especially Dorene Hinton.

So you see, I, Libby Sunberg, was not unfamiliar with the attention of young men. As soon as I reached puberty I noticed the ogling, leering even, as my nubile presence strolled the halls of Milbank, South Dakota high school. Fortunately, the ninth grade boys who at this stage of their development couldn't decipher their arms from their legs, had no idea how to assemble them into a coordinated attempt to even speak to me. All except one, who was a real pest and a bit frightening as he oozed against me in the locker bay. In self defense, I flat-handed him as hard as I could across the face, hard enough to leave a red mark but not deter his advances. Offended by my assault, he incited other boys to diss me, even call me derogatory names and make up stories about my sexual behavior, which they probably texted to who knows whom. What I was to discover was that I would encounter some of the same kind of creeps here in Buford Post.

The worst thing that happened took place at lunch. The upper class boys lined up against the wall and watched us sophomore girls pass, rating each one of us from one to ten until the teacher on lunchroom supervision discovered what was happening and broke up their disgusting party. I didn't know any of them yet, but I'd remember the most flagrant violators who hissed at the ones and two and cat called at the nines and tens. Wendy and I got cat calls, not that it mattered. We didn't acknowledge their juvenile behavior. What douches. I couldn't imagine what it must be like to be hissed at. Anyway it only happened once. Some of them even snapped photos on their smart phones. Dark.

So here we were in Buford Post, Wisconsin a thriving community of the Buford/Camden consolidated public schools, the Watering Hole Sports Bar and Restaurant, the Buford Post

National Bank, Lucy's Bar and Grill, an insurance agency, an Amoco Service Station, Bait Shop and Boat Rental owned by the Hintons, the Buford Millworks and Lumber Company, and the Odegaard Dairy and Cheese Factory.

Buford Post, Wisconsin is a little town that continued to grow, especially in the summer when tourists arrived to stay in the Swanson Resort of several cabins and restaurant that overlooks the rolling Mississippi as it meanders toward its New Orleans destination. No one would deny that the bucolic, river route on either side of the river from St. Paul, Minnesota through Hastings and the carved cliffs of Red Wing, past eleven mile Lake Pepin and Lake City and Reeds Landing on the Minnesota Side and Stockholm, Buford Post, Alma, and Nelson on the Wisconsin side is one of the most spectacular sites in the United States. Dotted with islands and backwater channels where every fresh water fish awaits the fisherman's bait and the river offers the peace that a boy just younger than I was then wrote many years ago. Well, not really a boy. It was Mark Twain narrating for Huckleberry Finn, an unwashed kid with a remarkable ability to bring his days on the river to life. From the first day I looked down on that river from where our home sits, I understood what natives love about it. It is beauty. It is peace. It is adventure.

But the town itself was a conundrum. In spite of the river's inspiration, the townspeople didn't always exhibit it in their behavior. It was like every other town, I guess, somewhat distant from itself, if you know what I mean. I had misgivings about the guys in this school, and rumors surrounded several of the girls. They probably thought I was a snob.

WENDY TOLD ME our biology teacher was new to Buford Post and to teaching. At the age of twenty-two, he, a recent science graduate from Southwest State University in Marshall, Minnesota, contracted for his first teaching job at BP. Not only was he handsome, single, energetic, and some might say charismatic, he made sure that his students understood the urgency of climate change. He encouraged action by individual citizens, social justice groups and, of course, the city, county, state and national legislative bodies. The urgency, he explained, was based on the continued burning of fossil fuels that causes an over abundance of carbon dioxide in our atmosphere. This biology class imported to help us, he explained, to understand the scientific principles fundamental to life on the planet—human, animal, and plant. "The first unit," he said, "will focus on the needs of plant life to survive in various habitats and what natural and human processes threaten their existence. From that introduction the course will proceed to show the interdependence of plant and animal life." He gave us a series of websites to explore to find our special interests in the subject. Wavy. I liked him. I knew I would love that class.

Both the course description and Mr. Russell's demeanor held my attention. I knew about climate change, of course, but I'd never thought about the urgency for developing solutions. I wanted to learn about it all as did most of my classmates. Wendy was especially eager and whispered to me, "Isn't he lit!" It wasn't a question. Wendy bubbled over with excitement for this course. I agreed totally, and so our friendship began, first from discussing biology lessons then to school issues and girlfriends and boys, and other teachers, and the homecoming festivities coming up in the next month. Of course, we exchanged phone numbers and texted back and forth constantly. She, like me, invited the attention of the upperclass males. Her braces would come off in the spring.

The conversation between us couldn't be more natural. Wendy had substance in spite of some frivolous interests. I mean who was perfect. I certainly wasn't and I'm not just saying that. Besides she played the oboe in the concert band, an instrument I considered nearly impossible to play because of its double reed. I played the clarinet, and pardon me for saying so, I played it pretty well. So we really hit it off. Soon we were planning social engagements and inviting other school friends, to whom she introduced me. (I learned how to use who and whom in my Milbank English class.)

One day at noon I filled my plate in the cafeteria line with chicken slices, French fries, baked beans and a cup of chocolate ice cream, a meal not exactly to my liking but filling. I would have preferred a green salad without onions and a dash of vinegar and olive oil dressing. The ice cream was fine, but I'd rather have a cup of strawberry yogurt. Tuesday was taco day. That was okay. I liked tacos, still do, when I'm not on a diet. From then on, however, I planned to bring my own lunches. No way would I eat the stuff in the vending machines.`

Leaving the line I searched for a place to sit among the boisterous students chowing down and saw Wendy sitting with a group of girls whom I recognized as the standoffish elitists fiddling with their phones between bites. No matter. I sat down beside Wendy who greeted me with a smile and leaned over to brush my shoulder when one of the crew commented, "Let's bounce." Almost in chorus the other four rose from the table, gathered their dishes, pocketed their phones and left, sporting a disdainful grin.

"What was that all about?" I asked, "They haven't even finished their meal. "Was that exit about me?"

"Oh, forget them. They're upset because Kurt Buford flirted with you," Wendy responded.

"Who's Kurt Buford?"

"You know the quarterback. He comes from a long line of Bufords who founded the town during the lumbering days. They started the sawmill four generations ago and passed it down to their sons up to the present. Look up the town website and you can learn all about the family. Kurt will most likely be the next generation owner. Recently, the Buford bank, operated by my father, loaned them the money for the expansion of their industry to include the construction company that makes yard barns from plywood and particle board, and green wood or cedar for sheds, mulch and decks to home owners throughout the area and much of Wisconsin. Recently they added the millworks designed to make double paned thermal windows.

"Really. You know a lot about it."

"Everybody does. That company is considered the backbone of the community."

"Good to know, but I've only talked to that guy once in the hall when he came smiling up to me and asked if I was coming to the game tomorrow night and I said I didn't know and that I wasn't much interested in football. He didn't know I played in the band."

"That was enough. A couple of The Kin saw that and spread the word that you were flirting with him."

"Well, I wasn't but maybe I should. He's very cute and seems sweet."

"Yeah, but looks can be deceiving."

If his looks are deceiving, I'm eager to be deceived." He was the perfect six feet in height, eyes blue as robin's eggs, that kind of turquoise blue, and wavy dirty blond hair long on top to curl over blended sides. His physique announced that he was a trained athlete with smooth arm muscles and I guessed six pack abs. I knew, I shouldn't be thinking about his bod, but give me a break. He was gorgeous. Besides I wasn't interested. Maybe later.

"So why were you sitting with them?" I asked. "They don't seem like your type."

"I'm not. They came to sit with me because they know that you and I are friends and they could diss you."

I chuckled then laughed out loud and shook my head in disbelief.

"So they have their heads up their butts because he introduced himself to me in the hallway. What skanks. You said, The Kin?"

"There are five of them, I think, an exclusive group, apparently leaving no room for anyone else. They've been together since grade school and often have parties in which they invite the most popular boys who enjoy the affections these girls offer. I don't know exactly what goes on, but I can guess. They don't have a good reputation, I can tell you that. They've been trying to get Kurt to join them. I don't know if he has. Some of his friends on the team have been to one or more of the shindigs. I know that."

"What about their parents? Don't they know what's going on?"

"I doubt it. They always have a party at a home when the parents are away, the parents assuming that because they are juniors and seniors in high school, they should be able to take care of themselves. Somebody stands guard with phone ready in case they arrive unexpectedly."

At noon the next day Wendy and I arranged to meet for the taco lunch. When I entered the cafeteria, I spotted the handsome quarterback sitting with his team mates chowing down while thumbing their phones. As I passed I said to Kurt, "I'm coming to the game tonight, so play well guys." I brushed past them but let my eyes linger on Kurt's. As I twisted away, I tossed a smile like a red rose toward them as they roared their approval. I imagined they were jostling Kurt about that as I pass.

"I saw that," Wendy commented as I joined her in line. "Oooh, you've done it now. You saw The Kin at the next table, didn't you."

"Oh, yes, it was for them."

"I'd go easy if I were you. They can be mean."

"I'm sure you're right, but I couldn't help it."

"Oh, boy, you'll be the loser in the game you're playing."

"Think so?"

"I think so"

"We'll see. Besides we have to be there because we're playing in the band."

"Of course."

The Buford/Camden Jacks won 14 to 7 over the Sterling Eagles. The band played the Jacks rouser to the tune of "Anchors Away." I played the notes but hadn't learned the words except for Rah, Rah, Rah, Go Jacks Go.

ON MONDAY I saw the word SLUT in black staring at me from the silver locker face in the sophomore section of the locker bay. I felt a scream building but I stopped it before it gathered strength. I didn't want a scene. I just wanted that ugly word gone. I texted Wendy. She convinced me to let the matter rest and ran for the custodian to take care of it. I was dumbfounded. I had thought my flirtation was harmless. Maybe not.

The custodian repainted the locker face before classes began, so very few students saw it. Still word spread like fire and by noon Kurt learned of the incident. He sought me out after my last class. How he knew it was math on the second floor I'd never know, but there he was, consoling me like a brother. It wasn't a brother I saw in him, but it was a tender gesture. He offered to drive me home rather than I take the school bus and stupid me, I agreed. I'd already forgotten what had produced the word on my locker.

"I'll find out who did this, and make sure nothing like this happens again," he promised. I thanked him as he drove me in his Ford Fusion from school to the outer edge of a nice middle class neighborhood of mostly two story box houses, some with screen porches, others open, on top of the bluff overlooking the river. My home had an open porch so wasn't much good at mosquito hour in the summer, but we had screened it in by when autumn arrived with leaves turning oak gold and maple scarlet. He left with a nod and a smile.

I sat for a while on the hanging swing and thought. I shouldn't have made the overture to Kurt and his football friends in front of the girls in the cafeteria. And now I allowed him to drive me home. What was I thinking? I ran through the faces at the table trying to decide who the sicko was who could do such a thing. Did she do it on her own or was she put up to it? I'd have to stay out of their way, but I wouldn't ignore Kurt. I liked him. He had his appeal. I texted Wendy, who warned me against him, but she didn't tell me why.

After a day like that I wished I was back in Milbank. I texted Sherry Willard, my best friend back there who I really missed. She and I did everything together. She's really smart so we got along. She introduced me to me to snapchat and texting, and she helped me establish a username. We promised not to share our names with anyone else unless we got permission from each other. I told her I wanted Wendy in. She said, OK. And Sherry included Jassy Johnson with my permission. Sherry was doing well. They spent most of their time together. Jassy played French horn and Sherry played bassoon. You had to be really smart to play either one of those instruments. I really missed Sherry.

The next day Wendy told me that Kurt was Dorene's bae, meaning boyfriend. They were "hanging out together." And he had been to at least one of the Kin festas. Had I misjudged him. Was he not the cool dude he seemed to be? Was he toying with me?

By afternoon most of the student body had heard of the incident though few had seen it. As I pulled my jacket from my locker, a girl from behind me said, "Libby?" and I recognized one of The Kin facing me. "I'm so sorry to hear about the gross word painted on your locker. You don't deserve that. I don't know who would do such a thing. I'm Tara Morrisey. I hope you don't think it was one of us." I was truly startled and didn't know what to say except, "Thank you." She turned and walked down the hall toward the outside door.

Was she telling the truth or was she the Kin's emissary sent to remove suspicion? She seemed legit. She wouldn't have had to tell me her name, but she did as if she wanted to be identified as "one of them." I was puzzled so I told Wendy about it who told Kurt who knew Tara and agreed that SHE wouldn't do anything like that. But any of the others? He didn't know. I studied his reaction carefully, trying to read him, hoping I could trust him and my assessment of him. Wendy told me that Tara was a Cheesehead, a real Cheesehead, not just a Packers fan. Her parents worked at the Odegaard Cheese Factory.

The next few days were without incident. The weather cooled, the trees painted the blue sky with their colors, and the daylight hours shortened. Football season was in full swing. The band, in our red and white uniforms, with gold arm tassels and red plumed helmets performed the opening and halftime shows for an appreciative audience. Wendy played the alto sax in marching band, but I stayed with the clarinet.

Biology class proved to be as interesting and challenging as I expected. I'd become convinced that global warming was the greatest threat to my generation and the planet. I was prepared to text my friends, write on Facebook, join marches, carry signs, and convince my elders to support candidates that promised action if elected.

The other issue that concerned several students here was the school shootings. In my sophomore American history class emotions roamed the political map among us and in our conversations about it with our parents most of whom were hunters and supported the NRA. Clearly we were worried about our future, whether it was safe to go to school. We wanted our leaders to do what was right for us. We were ready to make our voices heard in whatever ways we could. Mr. Ruiz taught us about civil disobedience and the price we might have to pay if we pursued it. Then, too, there was the price we would have to pay if we didn't.

One Thursday evening after an extra band practice on the football field to perfect the halftime show for the next night, Kurt approached me at the gate and asked to take me home. At first I declined but then he smiled and offered again in his soothing voice and I climbed into the Fusion that his dad insisted on buying because of his connection with the Ford dealer in LaCrosse. He insisted on walking me to the our front door and when I turned toward the door, he grabbed my arm and wheeled me around like a top into his arms and kissed me hard. Instead of returning his kiss, I repelled him, at first with a slight push backward, then a violent shove. This was not what I expected or wanted. It was not how I wanted to be treated. My attraction turned to sudden revulsion.

"Don't you dare do that again, ever, you understand," I yelled at him.

Kurt smiled then got the message, shook his head in disbelief, as if I had just refused the lottery, then left. Was I the first girl who had refused him? And why was he kissing me if Dorene was his bae?

I slipped passed my parents in the kitchen and climbed the stairs to my bedroom. I left it dark and peered out the window that faces the backyard. Something moved among the drooping leaves of the weeping willow, or was it a breeze causing the disturbance? From the front window I saw that the Ford had gone, so it wasn't Kurt. Then who? Perhaps, I imagined too much. I had to calm myself. I texted Wendy, but told her not to come over. I took several deep breaths and went down to dinner and sat in my usual place beside my older brother.

"How was practice?" Mom inquired as she continued preparing the meal. "Your father should be home soon. Can you wait?

"Good practice. I can wait."

"Are you okay?" Mom inquired. "You seem distracted."

Sorry, I'm fine, just tired. It's been a long day."

WHILE THE FOOTBALL team ran over their opponents, the band played the rouser and performed the halftime show at each home game. During the fifth week of the season the school administration, teachers and students prepared for the Homecoming festivities. I had several encounters with Kurt, mostly in the school corridors where he narrowed the space between us and then cozied up to Dorene at her locker or beside her in the lunch room. Whenever I came into his sight lines he gave me a smile and a wink as if Dorene were nowhere around. I didn't know what to make of him. One noon he brought his lunch and sat down across from me and Wendy and taunted us about our liberal politics that were mostly unwelcome in our community. Not true among the students, I pointed out, and we jousted about what good our action agenda would do. He wasn't against me exactly. Actually, he sided with me, or pretended to, but wasn't convinced of any action. I wondered if he was sincere, since he owned guns and liked to hunt for quail and deer.

"You can't even vote," he teased.

"Ya, but I can vote for Homecoming King, Do you think I should vote for you?"

"Well, sure, I'd like to be King, if you'd be my queen."

"Oh, but I'm just a wee little Sophomore, remember. Only seniors can be King and Queen. And Dorene is your queen."

"Ya, I suppose."

"Of course, Dorene," Wendy chimed in. She's got money."

"And don't forget good looks," Kurt sputtered. "She's a charmer."

"You should know. She charms you often enough."

"Aw, we're just friends. I can't help it if she hits on me. What am I supposed to do? Tell her to get lost?"

"That would be a start," Wendy sneered.

At home I flopped into the sofa and stared at the ceiling. I imagined Kurt, the King, and Dorene Hinton, the Queen, riding in the Cadillac convertible loaned for the Homecoming parade by Dorene's dad and Dorene snuggling up to Kurt. Yuck, what did he see in her, except she was thirsty. Maybe that was all, and he didn't see that in me. And then clad as a warrior in his football uniform he'd present her with the crown at halftime and seat her in the queen's chair in the box seat and kiss her on the cheek. Ick. I had to admit I was jealous in spite of how repulsed I was by him. I couldn't stand Dorene. Why? Because she had Kurt and I didn't, even though I didn't want him. What was the matter with me? I didn't even have time for him. Still he attracted me. But there were others. If I wanted a boyfriend I could make my choice. "Forget him," I prodded myself.

Of course, they'd be king and queen. She was alluring with her silky naturally blond hair, slightly tanned soft skin and eyes that invited romance. And she knew how to walk to demand attention. I hated her.

ONE SATURDAY TWO weeks before Homecoming, Kurt in a by-the-way sort of posture, suggested to me, "Why don't you be my date at the homecoming dance. We went silent. Then Wendy sighed, "Kurt are you nuts?"

"No, I'm serious. We can't let a few jealous girls control our lives." Kurt responded.

I said nothing for the moment as I considered an appropriate response. Then Wendy interjected, "You have to be the Queen's partner at the dance, you know."

"Right, but I can still dance with you, Libby."

"And cause a stink. Wouldn't that be like the King abandoning his throne?"

"Who gives a damn about royalty? It's nonsense."

"Careful. It's tradition. You don't want to upset tradition." Wendy blurted.

"But I'm going to dance with Libby."

"I can't dance."

"Neither can I. All we have to do is hold each other."

"You mean so Dorene and all The Kin can see."

"And the whole student body."

Wendy piped in, "Then you can go back to your seat and flirt with the "Queen.""

"And what makes you think I want to hold you?" I sneered.

After all he just wanted to use me to make Dorene jealous. Still he asked me to be his date. I didn't know if this was his game or if he was truly interested in me.

Of course The Kin would be dancing, putting on a show. Mona Thomas' parents operated the dance studio, so all those girls could dance—and would with all the guys. And Dorene would sit on her throne.

And that was exactly how Homecoming went, just as predicted, complete with snobbery on both sides and tension in relationships. Everyone watched as the King stepped down from his throne, walked across the dance floor, held his hand out to me and led me onto the floor. Everyone watched as if we were the bride and groom opening the dancing for the wedding reception, except that the evening was well under way and this event was inappropriate to the teacher coordinator of the dance and a few of the planning committee. Still most agreed that Kurt and I made a lovely pair. I was beginning to think so, too, even as I resisted his embrace.

The dance was sponsored by the Chamber of Commerce with several members and parents supervising. Red and white streamers and carnations decorated the gym to make the room look like a Valentine's Day event, without the hearts. The Jacks had won the game by several touchdowns over the Ferguson Hawks, that had won only two games all fall. As predicted The Kin were popular with the guys who waited in line to skank with each and to learn a lesson or two. It was fun to watch, I had to admit. Mona asked Kurt to dance and he complied doing his best to follow her feet. Fascinating. Then he asked me to dance again. I tried to dissuade him because I knew the whole student body and sponsors would stop to watch us fumble. After all he was the football hero and I, the new sophomore package. But he led me onto the floor as the DJ spun Taylor Swift's "Safe and Sound." At least it was a slow enough number for us to keep control of our feet. Others joined us by the third phrase and things seemed normal. I allowed him to pull me in. I suppose I should have felt honored.

THE NEXT MONDAY as Wendy and I walked home from school, Wendy mused, "What if it wasn't one of The Kin that painted that word," Could anyone else have it in for you?"

"I have no idea. I haven't even talked to any guys except Kurt and a few in biology class. One kid, Billy Olson, was my lab partner when we dissected a frog. He's really smart and kind. I like him. He's a boy I can talk to. I'd forget that locker incident altogether if I didn't think someone is watching me."

"You haven't told me about that. Have you seen anyone following you?"

"No and I don't know if there is or if it its my imagination."

"After that filth painted on your locker, you're bound to be a little jumpy," Wendy commented.

"I suppose, but I don't like the feeling." I thought Wendy felt it, too.

Suddenly Kurt pulled his Ford over and stopped beside us walking and offered us a ride. Wendy gave me a dissenting look, then gave in and hopped in the back seat. She left the passenger seat for me. It was too late to say no, so once more I was in jeopardy. Dammit, Wendy. I tried to act casual and uninterested, but I knew I wasn't successful. How could I be?

Kurt dropped Wendy off at the Westin front door then drove me, although I thought I'd rather walk, the two miles to my home. On the doorstep, he paused and looked into my eyes. I avoided making eye contact, I was afraid both that he might kiss me or he might not. He took my hand and said," I enjoyed dancing with you. You move very well."

Then he pecked me on the cheek.

Maybe I'd taught him some manners. Maybe he respected me after all.

"Goodnight," I whispered. "Thank you. I'll see you tomorrow."

"You're really wavy," he said.

I laughed, "So are you." I didn't go inside but waited for him to drive away. Then I crossed the upper road to the pathway that runs along the bluff.

Our house faces west on the east side of the upper road that rises north of town and winds its way south for access to the several homes on the bluff and then descends to meet the main road through town. West of that upper road is a foot path that meanders along the bluff and opens from time to time to a screened gazebo where walkers can pause to overlook the river for some miles north and south. There are three gazebos authorized by the town council and built by Buford Lumber. Townspeople and tourist alike enjoy the three mile walk and the scenic stopovers.

When I felt confused or down or both I often walked that pathway and sat in one of the gazebos to allow the soft flow of the river to sooth me. It spoke to me in a language I had come to understand, a language that I knew many of the locals know as well. In those moments I felt a part of them and less confused. That night under the bright three quarter moon I allowed myself to muse. The river shone between the darkened hillsides. Lights from barges outlined their length as they floated silently through the night. In the gazebo closest to my home I wished I could experience the peace I often felt here, but not tonight. After a few minutes I walked the short distance home and climbed the stairs to my bedroom. I looked out the window east over the dark vineyard that extends forty-five acres. It seemed like years since our move from Milbank to Buford Post when my parents convinced my brother John and I that their radical shift in life's plan would be an exciting adventure. John was all for it. I liked the idea but I didn't want to leave my friends.

I couldn't sleep, dreaming of Kurt and his lips on my ear. It still tingled. Then it occurred to me that the night might not be over for him. Maybe he went from me to Dorene. Damn, I wished I knew what was happening with him and with ME. Finally I slept, a restless sleep, as if my angels were arguing.

Except for Wendy and my teachers, Mr. Russell and Mr. Ruiz, I didn't know if I would like it here in Buford Post. I texted Sherry some photos I'd taken of the River and the school and, of course, I included Wendy, but no one else, not yet.

I thought of the family conversations we had had around the fire place on winter nights in our Milbank home. We could have those conversations here, too, I knew, and we would, but I remembered the summers there. In summer Milbank was a flowering, lush place of a variety of trees and the Hartford State Park and Big Stone Lake nearby for hiking and fishing. Our family often sought adventures in those places among the trees and water. Dad, John and I fished the lake from time to time as well as the Missouri River. I tell you these things so you know that it wasn't easy to leave a lovely place and good friends even though, as I said, there were creeps to deal with.

We took summer trips, too. I remember the one to California some years ago now where we spent a day in Disneyland, then drove north along the Pacific Coastal Highway, stopped off in Santa Barbara and the Santa Inez wine area. Mom and Dad loved wine and had been fascinated with the wine making process for years. John and I drank Mellow Yellow or Fanta, but we liked the atmosphere and the acres of vineyards. We didn't mind that we stopped in the Pasa Robles area then drove along the frightening and beautiful Big Sur, stayed in cheap motels, as cheap as you can get in the summer in California, mostly Budget or Motel Six, which was fine because it was just for sleeping. Then, of course, Sonoma and Napa Valley. Dad gathered all he could on their wines and bought a few bottles of red to age at home and white to drink with our evening meals. Mom told us many times to put our smart phones away and look at the scenery. We did when it was spectacular which was most of the time. But I had to text Sherry, too, you know. When we stopped for gas or lunch I'd find a quiet place to call Sherry just to hear her voice.

After the stimulus of several wineries in different parts of California, Dad had thoughts that he didn't share with us until one weekend in Minneapolis when we visited his parents. Dad had brought a Pasa Robles red to serve with the meal, but Dad's father, Lief, offered him another red with which to compare, not disclosing its origin. Unbeknown to my parents, they sipped on a delicious Minnesota wine grown, fermented, bottled and sold from the Cannon River Winery. Both Mom and Dad loved it. Dad's father, Lief, had taken an interest in the adventurous new vintners in Minnesota and Wisconsin ever since the University of Minnesota Agriculture Department had developed hardy hybrid grapes that could withstand the severe northern climate and the subsequent proliferation of wineries in the upper Midwest. At the dinner table to enhance the dinner salad, t-bone streaks, mashed potatoes, green beans, they tasted the palatable wines fermented from the Marquette grape. It had the body of a Cabernet and the fruity spicy bite of a Syrah, I was told. Delicious and surprising since the Sunbergs had only expected good vintners to come from California, especially Napa Valley. "Not true anymore," Lief said. "Now with the help of cross breeding, wine makers can produce good wines in many climate zones including the Mississippi River Valley that has proven to excel."

"Let's do it," Maggie and Dan enthused together reading each others' minds.

They looked at each other and laughed. That was it. The new adventure had scored a higher mark than the highways of the U.S. or exotic flights to Tahiti or Japan. Neither would settle on those anyway. Dan had Europe in mind, but that could wait. His father warned that to start a grape farm, as he called it, would take time, study and planning. You didn't just stick a few plants in the ground and wait for the fruit to appear.

"If you do it right and if you have patience, you can develop a distinct bouquet that will entice palates for miles around." Leif Sunberg emphasized, "Kari and I would love to help you get started. I mean financially. No sticking plants in the ground for me. I've done enough digging." As a retired architect he had often worked side by side with contractors to watch his project develop.

From that weekend of wine and baseball the Sunbergs started on a plan. It would take a long time to educate themselves about the nuances of wine making, but they needn't hurry. Both Dad and Mom engaged in vintner philosophies, in the successes, in failures and the whys and wherefore of each. They studied the process and considered the risks and learned all they could about the wine industry. Mom with her accounting background could calculate the financial risk and Dad would learn the agricultural complications, a more difficult task for an ex-social studies teacher. Since they knew ignorance threatened their success, they attacked with both mental barrels, each wielding a shotgun of hope aimed at an intangible nemeses that might circle above them. They had time to plan.

ON TUESDAY AS I was leaving Biology class with Wendy, Tara Morrissey approached me. "I want you to know I'm not a part of The Kin any more. I'm not like them. They do things I can't do and hit on guys I don't like. I mean, the football players are all right, mostly, but those out-of-towners are creeps. Most important is that I know you and Wendy are co-leaders of the Science Club that's focusing on global warming. I want to be part of that. I have a couple of friends who are interested, too. May I join you?"

"Of course," Wendy and I shouted at once.

"Do other Kin feel the same way?" I asked.

"I don't know. I haven't been hanging out with them lately. They've snubbed me because I refused to go along with some of their antics."

"Like what," Wendy probed.

"I'd rather not talk about it. Just know that I'm not a part of them any more. I don't do what they do."

If curiosity could kill a cat, Wendy was on her ninth life, but she let it go. I just shook my head. My curiosity was more about whether any of them had plans for me. I had learned that Dorene Hinton was their leader, the one that pressured the others to conform to her actions, and Kurt was attached to her.

On the other hand, the science club was gaining recognition. The members, several of whom were in the biology class and several juniors and seniors agreed with the club initiative and were part of creating the club agenda. The upperclassmen were especially helpful in that regard having more experience in establishing guidelines. They decided that the focus would be first on learning about the effects of global warming; second on exploring the initiatives of other action organizations to link up with, and third to initiate and take part in actions to influence those in power to make necessary changes including marches, sit-ins, e-mails, facebook entries, etc. How was that for an agenda. Yeah. The science club soon gained the interest of other students and because of them their parents and civic leaders as well. Not all were in support. Some, in fact, were in serious contention. Not all of the students were supportive either, among them The Kin. Wendy and I were chatting and texting now. She thought the Kin were a chatting clan, but she didn't know who was in it.

Earl Hinton, Dorsey's father, served on the school board with Marvin Coleman and five women. That meant the men needed to solicit the votes of the women to advance their agendas for which they often faced opposition since the men wanted to curb expenses and promote the athletics budget while slighting academics, especially the arts. Coleman agreed with Hinton's school board agenda and general conservative politics, but he supported the drama department because his daughter Millie was a star actor as a junior along with other members of the Kin. She, too, showed her discomfort with the attention I was getting as I continued to acquire support for the climate change effort. Clearly, The Kin were losing the popularity contest to me, a sophomore, who was more interested in my cause than in my popularity. Perhaps, Dorene thought she could entice me to join them, nullify my efforts and leave her in charge of me. No way.

Before we moved here Dan, my father, was teaching social studies at Milbank High School, and Maggie, my mother, served as an accountant for the Colby Cheese Factory. Roy and Elaine Anderson became their closest friends who were constant competitors in four handed cribbage and trips to Sioux Falls and even to Minneapolis to see the Twins play in the Dome. Their daughter Maia, a year younger than I, had her own best friends, but we did some things together. The Andersons have a cabin up near Riverton, Wisconsin on Boom Lake, a swelling of the Wisconsin River. They spent several weeks during the summer there and still do. They had often entertained us for a few days where we all enjoyed the lake activities. So when my parents proffered the vintner adventure, the Andersons loved the idea and promised the use of their cabin from time to time as Dad explored land options further south along the Mississippi River. Their cabin wasn't convenient, but easier and more pleasant than a five hour trip back to Milbank. Of course they had the option to stay with Dad's parents in Minneapolis as well. In either case they had like-minded companions willing to offer ideas and maybe too much advice on the search process.

When they found the most ideal piece of forty acres near Buford Post, they hired an oenologist from Fountain City to put his stamp of approval on their selection and to advise them of initial procedures. So after thirteen years of teaching in Milbank High School and accounting at the Cheese Factory we moved to our new acreage and home. The serendipity of it is that Buford Post boasted the home of the Odegaard Dairy and Cheese Factory and offered a lucrative accounting job for Mom. Our future seemed to drop from the sky, i.e. if Buford Post proved to be a livable place.

By October, and two months into my fifteenth year, we had settled into our new house adjacent to our property, tilled the fields, only ten acres to start, installed the irrigation system, and planted the vines. We expected with proper pest control to have a few grapes in the fall but not a real harvest until the following year. I say, we, because I felt a part of this project even though I had not invested any of myself into it yet. But I would. And my brother had. In fact, with his degree in accounting and economics from St. Olaf College and his enthusiasm for this new adventure, he would be the captain of this new industry as president of the family business. Not every young man could get such a fascinating job right out of college. Of course, he would make no decisions against our parents' wishes.

Our forty-five acres of land on top of the bluff runs eastward across the sandy loam fields appropriate for raising grapes along the river. There we transformed the brick house built in the early 1900s into our three bedroom home and a wine tasting parlor. My parents have a first floor bedroom and John and I each had a room upstairs.

Behind and east of the house a hundred yards we built a winery complete with the aluminum fermenting vats and oak storage barrels for the wines that flowered from the hybrid grapes suitable to the harsh climate. Below my window was a beautiful weeping willow tree and a majestic oak from which a swing hung from a lower branch. It's still there after five years. It was a lovely vista. I hoped things would go well for us in our new venture and in this town.

THE HINTONS, WHERE most of the teen parties were held, own their 3000 square feet, two story, four bedroom home with three car garage on the North edge of town. Back then the garage housed a 2009 Lincoln, a Ford Ranger and recently purchased 2007 Ford Mustang for Dorene to run around in. The rec room on the lower level was the party room with pool table, air hockey game, pin ball machine, a 60 inch Samsung TV equipped with several Wii games and leather recliners with cup holders and built in massagers, a Whirlpool steel two door refrigerator with water and ice maker, and, of course, a bar with sink and cupboards. Still there was room for dancing to the blue tooth juke box that offered whatever playlist we buttoned in. Many nights The Kin gathered in this pleasure palace with male friends, some out-of-towners, for an evening's entertainment. The parents, either upstairs or out for the evening, ignored the activities assuming innocent fun.

One midweek afternoon Rusty Pearson, a linebacker on the football team, stopped at Minnies' for a burger and fries with Kurt, his best friend. Minnie, not an intentional eavesdropper, eavesdropped and passed her gossip on to her daughter Myra who told Wendy who told me. I repeat it here as accurately as I can. Rusty said, "I'm not attending another of Dorene's parties. You were there. You know what goes on. After the dancing, it got pretty hot, too hot for me. You and Dorene disappeared somewhere. I'm guessing the bedroom. Before I had time to think, Rosemary had me on the couch with her hands all over me. At first I responded, but then I rejected her advances. I told her I liked her but didn't want to do whatever she had in mind. She lay back disappointed then made another attempt. But I was on my feet. I smiled and said she was a nice kid but I had to get home. So I left. I don't know how far the adventures went after I left," he whispered, "but I can guess. I'm quite sure that if I had stayed, I would have had a new experience, if you know what I mean. Tanner stayed. I haven't dared to talk to him about the rest of the evening. And what about you?"

"Shit man, you're taking this too seriously. It was just a lot of fun. The girls wanted some romance and we gave it to them."

"Ya, well I was tempted to stay and see what happened. It would have been easy to go along. I don't know how I resisted. It must be that my mother was praying for me. She always does."

"Mine, too. I wish she'd let up."

"No you don't."

"No, I don't. Sometimes when the meal is before you, you want to eat.

"I was about to have dessert before the main course."

"What does that mean?"

"I don't know, but I knew the serving would leave a bad taste in my mouth that would never go away."

"I think Tanner may have had at least a spoonful."

"He probably already knows how fattening she can be."

Minnie came with the hamburgers and fries and smiling like she had downed a cup of Double Chocolate Crunch said, "Enjoy your lunch, guys."

Paying no attention to her, which was what she hoped, they didn't bother with a thanks.

More rumors. I'm not revealing the source. In the locker room after basketball practice, Tanner, a six foot forward, sat on the bench across from the lockers still naked after drying off. Kurt, toweling, stood beside him. "Hey, Tanner, you seemed a little sluggish today. Anything wrong?"

"Naw, just a little tired. I didn't get much sleep last night."

"So something is wrong."

"Well, sort of. You know Rosy Masters."

"Yeah, I know her. She was at the party Saturday night."

"Well, I was dancing with her at Dorene's last Friday after the game, and she decided she was for me and that I should make a commitment to her and I didn't want to."

"So just tell her you like her but don't want any strings."

"Somehow she thinks I owe her."

"Do you?"

"Maybe."

"I see."

Neither spoke for a long minute. Then Kurt suggested, "You don't owe her. Whatever happened she was as much responsible as you. Right?"

"Well, sure, but—"

"But nothing. You're a good guy. Don't go there. Don't get dragged in."

"But what if…" Tanner quit.

"Shit, man. Stay away."

"Yeah, I know."

When they got up to leave, Kurt put his arm around Tanner's shoulder and said, "When she cozies up to you again, apologize for your behavior. You'll know what to say."

"What makes you think so?"

"Just talk straight down."

"And what should I say?" That I wanted her, I wanted to have sex with her and now I don't? That's the truth. I really fucked up."

"I guess you could say that."

"You're gnarly, man. You'll be all right."

"Hope so."

"What about you and Dorene, Kurt?

"Everything's okay."

Yeah?

Yeah.

"And what about that sophomore gem. Hmmm? Seems like you want the meal and the dessert like Rusty said. That may be good cuisine but not so good when it comes to women as if I should know." That was the end of the conversation.

I learned of this conversation and several others months later when it all started coming down: the following conversation of town leaders, for example.

AT THE OCTOBER meeting of the Lions' Club to which Hinton, Coleman, and Buford were members, the most pressing addition to the new business focused on the new biology teacher, Mr. Hayward Russell, who seemed to be challenging the economic well being of the community. That is to say, he was riling the students into a kind of frenzy over climate change. In the discussion that followed chairman Sullivan brought the item to the floor, Buford pointed out that while he was aware that climate change was an issue, he felt the way in which Russell pursued it threatened some of the vital community interests, particularly his business. Hinton didn't see that Russell's agenda impacted his business specifically, but pointed out that if Russell's initiative were to succeed in halting the delivery of oil to refineries it could. Others spoke in support for the status quo. Mr. Coleman suggested that one of them, specifically Mr. Hinton, should talk with Mr. Russell and ask him to tone it down. None of them wanted any protests, sit ins, or demonstrations of any kind here in Buford Post or Buffalo County or the state legislature. And what about the young upstart, Libby Sunberg? Westin said he would suggest to Dan that he rein in his daughter. They all agreed that the Sunberg winery would be an asset to the town and would bring in tourists to sample the wine, spend money in their restaurants, buy gas, cheese, and maybe even rent a fishing boat or houseboat for an expedition in the back waters of the big river. The members agreed on what was good for the town and adjourned feeling confident they had a plan of merit.

As polite as my dad is, he rejected Westin's gentle nudge to ask his daughter to go easier on the global warming consequences, because he agreed with me. To him climate change was a real threat and, as matter-of-factly as he could, suggested the Lions' Club as well as the Chamber of Commerce make a public statement to that effect. Westin, who agreed with him, suggested, however, that being the new family and welcomed business in town that he should adapt to the local perspectives on things. After all, this was a town of established businesses that had succeeded on their agreed upon perspectives. Dad apologized if he had offended his solicitor, but was firm in his convictions. Also he appreciated the financial support the Buford Bank had given him as well as his friendship. Westin admitted he didn't want to bring the subject up to him and was sorry he did. He said, in fact, "I admire your daughter's enthusiasm."

Coleman had no success with Mr. Russell, who was adamant and passionate. Instead of conceding any point, he presented statistics and consequences of pollutants and carbon emissions and begged him to bring his message to the town officials. He said he wanted this town, now his town, to be a model for effecting necessary change and support the initiatives to save the planet.

Upon hearing via the grapevine of the unsuccessful solicitations, the Lions' called a special meeting to address the situation. The meeting adjourned without a plan. Clearly, the town leadership felt threatened and would not accept rejection easily. All of this information I pulled out of my Dad in pieces by inquiring, cajoling, and playing Daddy's girl with him. He knew what I was up to, but, I guess he thought I was mature enough to know this information.

Since that autumn was the first after the planting of the Frontenac red and gris and the Baco Noir grape vines, no grapes were ready to harvest, not until the following year, if all went well. So that was our year to prepare and invest in the future crop. Planting and tending were tasks for us new vintners which involve protecting the vines from the winter cold by covering them with an insulation. The remainder of the irrigation system and planting would have to wait until spring. The preparation took time and energy from each member of the family, each of which was eager to participate, including me. Each saw this business as an exciting new adventure. I, in particular, thought of it as living off the earth, a healthy way of life that depended on healthy soil and air.

In spite of the ecumenical Thanksgiving service held at 10 a.m. at the Our Saviors Lutheran Church in Cameron, just seven miles up the road from the town center of Buford Post, the passing of blessing and prayers of thanksgiving didn't seem to alleviate the tension that had been building in the community. It's an ancient church, at least by my standards, built in the fifties out of limestone and stretches upward to create a modified gothic feel. It seats about 300 people, a facility large enough for the growing community of Lutherans. Yes, the Presbyterian Bufords were there, and the Catholic Hofstedders, and, of course, the pastors and priest of the three churches, and the Lutheran Westins and Odegaards. Although not affiliated with any church, we Sunbergs were there as well, in thanksgiving for our new home, community, and good fortune in establishing our vineyard. We greeted each other respectfully and wished each other well, then departed to our homes and Thanksgiving dinner.

It became clear among the youth and townspeople that the community was divided over the perspectives brought by newcomers, we Sunbergs especially me, and the new biology teacher Hayward Russell. But no one anticipated the severity of the disagreements until Mr. Russell didn't appear in class on the Monday after Thanksgiving. When the principal's secretary tried to contact him by phone, he apologized for not calling in sick and hoped to be in class the next day. He was under the weather, he said. Since he hadn't been absent before and was new to the school, she accepted his apology and reminded him of proper protocol when it was necessary to be absent and thought he sounded more distressed than sick. She told her boss, who decided to investigate.

No one answered when he knocked on the front door of Russell's two bedroom apartment in a four plex a couple of blocks from the town center, so he called Russell's number on his smart phone. He answered but he preferred not to have any visitors. The principal wouldn't accept that answer.

"What's wrong? You're not sick. Something's wrong."

"Yes, something's wrong. I got beat up."

"You, what? Will you please let me in?"

"Yes, come in. The door's unlocked."

Russell sat on the sofa of his apartment with head in his hands. Principal Gregory pulled up a chair from the kitchen and sat across from him. He could see the teacher's swollen face from behind his protecting hands.

"Who did this to you?"

"I don't know. They attacked me after Ruiz dropped me off from the Watering Hole as I was about to enter my condo. As Ruiz drove off two men jumped me. I think it was two, but it happened so fast I can't be sure." He removed his hands from his face to reveal a very black eye and cut cheeks that had swollen to hide his bloody nose. "I managed to stumble back to my front door and get the key in the lock. My ribs hurt."

"Were they after money?"

"No, they said I should quit feeding kids crazy ideas."

"What crazy ideas have you been feeding them?

"I suppose about climate change."

"Ah, maybe, that issue is a sore spot with a few of the town leaders. So what are we going to do about you?"

"I don't know. I can't come to school looking like this and I won't look like me for a while."

"How about if we send you home because your mother has taken suddenly ill and you have to tend to her. We'll put you on temporary leave with full pay."

"You would do that?"

"Yes, where do you need to go?"

"Cedar Rapids, IA."

"Can you drive?"

"Yes, I can drive."

"It's best you leave asap and avoid seeing anybody. In the meantime, I'll investigate to see who did this to you. Who are your supporters I can talk to?"

"The Sunbergs, for sure, and Don Westin, but he may be pulled in different directions."

"You may be right. He's a friends of the Bufords."

"Talk to Libby, Sunberg's daughter. She's been the most vocal on the global warming subject, she and Wendy Westin. I think her father supports her effort."

"Ok, I'll stand with you. I believe in your cause. So does the superintendent. That's why we hired you. There's something more going on here than disagreements about climate change. You heal up and come back ready to carry on. The kids love you and they should. You have their future at heart. Take care." As he returned to school, he prepared the message to distribute to the staff and students.

"We're sorry to say that Mr. Russell will be on leave indefinitely due to his mother's illness. Offer your prayers if you are so inclined." That message he delivered over the school PA system, both to inform the student body and to entice the perpetrators of this crime against his teacher to leak a contradiction that could implicate the offenders.

I thought it odd that the principal would make such an announcement. Generally, the substitute teacher made such a statement to the students in class. Why the whole student body? No information appeared on the electronic board in the lunch room. Wendy didn't think much of it, but both of us would miss him deeply. No substitute could inspire the way he did.

In social studies class, Mr Ruiz said nothing about it, which seemed strange because Ruiz and Russell were friends, closest in age among the teachers and both single. Two young female teachers offered them some female companionship from time to time, but they hadn't coupled up as a far as anyone had observed. Some speculated that these two male teachers were more than just friends, but most discounted that.

I wondered if Ruiz knew anything about Russell's mother's illness. I asked him as I left class about her. Had she been sick long? How serious was it? And how long did he expect him to be absent? To which Ruiz stammered an "I don't know. He didn't tell me about her illness." He seemed puzzled as he spoke as if not quite making sense of the situation. Then he confided, "He didn't say anything when I was with him Sunday night." He stopped, realizing it was inappropriate to tell his students more. But he had said enough to convince Wendy and me that the principal's story was a cover up.

After school Wendy and I walked to Russell's condo to investigate. Maybe he was there. He wasn't, of course. We were about to leave when Wendy stooped to the outdoor mat and said, "Look." I bent down beside her and we examined the brown spot beside the mat on the concrete. "Do you think this is what I think it is?" Wendy whispered afraid of what she was thinking.

"If you think its blood, I agree. And here's another. He was hurt when he unlocked his door."

"Ruiz must know something about this." Wendy speculated.

"Or maybe he doesn't. That's why he seemed so puzzled."

"Should we talk to Mr. Gregory? I think he's hiding something."

"Why would he talk to us?"

"Maybe he won't. Maybe he'll stay with his story."

"Or maybe his manner will reveal something."

"Come in, girls," Mr. Gregory smiles as he invites us to sit. "How can I help you?"

We liked him. Everybody did. He seemed to be truly interested in his staff and students. We knew he had a special affection for Mr. Russell, that was why we needed to probe.

I began. "We're concerned about Mr. Russell's mother. She must have taken an unexpected turn."

"I appreciate your concern. We're hoping for her return to health, so that he can be back with us soon. I'll let everyone know as soon as I have new information. Thanks for your concern. Is there anything else.?

We looked at each other, then at the floor, then I looked right into Gregory's eyes and said, We found blood on his doorstep."

Gregory fidgeted with the papers on his desk, then tried to hide his agitation, "I'm sure you must be mistaken. Now if there's nothing else, I have business to attend to."

We left, convinced more than ever that Gregory was hiding the truth, which made us more anxious. Something had happened to our favorite teacher and Gregory knew about it.

WENDY AND I decided to play detective. In fact, we had already begun. It was back to Ruiz.

"So, you said Mr. Russell didn't say anything to you about his mother being sick when you brought him home. May we ask where you were together last Sunday night?" I probed after class on Wednesday sounding the part.

"Aren't you the little detectives?" He pretended to be light hearted. "It's not an appropriate question but you've aroused my curiosity. We were at the Watering Hole watching the Packers' game that they won 20 to 10.

"Where's that?"

"Of course you wouldn't know. It's a sports' bar on the riverfront where people hang out."

"What happened there?"

"Nothing. We left and I took Hayward home. That was it. Evidently, his sister called from Cedar Rapids to inform him about his mother's illness after I left, and he packed up and left."

"Wouldn't he let you know that?" Wendy continued.

"It does seem strange to me, too." Clearly Ruiz was puzzled.

"So you know nothing about the blood on his doorstep?" Libby pressed him.

"What?"

"Yes, You want to see?" That was Wendy.

Ruiz seems dazed. It was 3 p.m. and Ruiz said, "Let's go." Not thinking about what it might look like if people saw him, a teacher, transporting two sophomore girls in his car.

At the Russell doorstep we saw nothing. The supposed drops of blood had been scrubbed away. The scrubbing was obvious.

"The drops were here earlier," Wendy exclaimed.

"It's clear that something was washed away right here and here," Ruiz pointed to the spots. "I don't know what to make of this. But something is wrong. Hayward must be hurt."

"Maybe he didn't go to his mother's at all." I suggested.

"I'm going to call him. I should have done so right away to wish him and his mother well." He pressed on Mr. Russell's number. It kept ringing but no answer. "I'll have to get in touch with his mother via the Cedar Rapids phone directory." He found an Elizabeth Russell and called her number. She answered, "Hello, who's calling?"

My name is Lincoln Ruiz. I'm a teacher friend of Hayward. Is he there?"

"No, he's teaching in Buford Post. Why would he be here? Is everything all right?"

"I'm sure it is. I hope your health improves."

"I'm doing fine for an old woman. Hayward intends to spend time here over Christmas."

"Wonderful. He'll love that time with you. I have to go now. Take care."

We three sat in the car stunned. The next stop, the principal. He usually stayed at the school until five, so this should be a good time to investigate. Now there were three detectives.

Principal Gregory admitted that he covered up the beating for several reasons of which he could only think of one, that he wanted to keep people from knowing Russell had been in a fight. Russell looked terrible, Gregory said, but he didn't think he was badly hurt and would heal in a few days. "However, he should be in Cedar Rapids by now and his mother should have known he was coming unless he didn't want her to see him in his condition. That must be it. He went to a motel."

But Ruiz informed him that Russell didn't answer his phone. Maybe it was time to inform the police. Or maybe to hire a private investigator and where would they get one around Buford Post?

"I think we have our own detectives here," He nodded to us.

Then the horrible news arrived on the evening television news from LaCrosse. A man who lived along the highway 35 south of Alma saw what he thought was a VW Jetta miss a curve and plunge over the embankment into the river. He ran to see the result and could only see the back bumper above the water, so he called the police.

Shortly thereafter the Wisconsin Highway Patrol raced to the location and, as the man said, discovered Hayward Russell's VW Jetta submerged with only its tail lights visible above the water. The wrecking crew arrived and found Russell inside. It wasn't clear what could have caused him to lose control of his car. The three inch snow fall just before Thanksgiving had completely melted so the roads were clear now. No skid marks indicated no attempt to brake the vehicle. A protective barrier might have stopped it if there had been one, but Buffalo County hadn't felt one necessary since the shoulder was wide enough. None of the investigators committed to a cause of the accident, at least not yet, maybe when the final report was in after an autopsy.

Later that night I heard the news confirming their earlier report on the LaCrosse WXOW TV Station. Of course, I was devastated and I was certain this event was no accident. Someone must have been chasing him. That could be the reason he lost control of his car. He was driving too fast around the curves. Or was there something in the roadway? The man said it happened about noon.

Principal Gregory informed Russell's mother and his sister who lived with her in Cedar Falls. The body was sent to a funeral home there where the home official would make arrangements for the memorial service. As much as Wendy and I, our parents, Ruiz, and Principal Gregory cared about him, none of us decided to attend. This time Ruiz took charge. He conferenced with the investigators and asked them if any foul play was suspected. They had no such evidence. When the autopsy report came in, it concluded that Russell died from a brain hemorrhage or aneurism that killed him before his car plunged downward. He did not die from the fall or from drowning. Conclusion: an accident. No one tried to explain the battered face, assuming it occurred in the accident, no one except we detectives who were sure the beating he received caused the aneurism. For now we would say nothing but would keep our eyes and ears open.

On Tuesday, the day following the news, students were in school as usual with the same substitute teacher for biology. She was a competent, pleasant, and empathetic woman who often subbed in the school. Half of the biology students that day were too sullen to learn while others were hardly aware anything had happened. The sub had trouble keeping control of the smart phones.

THINGS WERE DIFFERENT now that Hayward Russell was gone. The atmosphere of the school hovered like a dark cloud over the classrooms, the gymnasium, even the counselors' offices and the administration. For a school run on an uplifting morning greeting to drag its feet through the day was saddening and alarming. The electronic board had its usual charming pep talks and feel good quotes. It seemed as if the terrible event that had taken place two, then two weeks, then a month beyond Christmas into the heart of the winter faded into the past or for some simmered on the back burner. The truth seemed buried with no hope of resurrection. As far as I know, only the perpetrators and Wendy, Ruiz, and Gregory and I knew of the beating. All others believed he was on his way to tend to his sick mother.

Relationships began to change. Dorene, who had never acknowledged my presence actually confided that Hayward Russell was a real loss to the school. She thought he was a little overboard with his climate change agenda, but she liked him and she admired me for taking up the cause. She even invited me to one of her parties, to which I responded with a smile and a thank you, but needed to know more about it. She asked for my phone number and I reluctantly I gave it.

Dorene asked me to think it over without offering further information and said she would invite Wendy, too. Why the turn around? I didn't know. Nor did Wendy when she mentioned to me the invitation she received. Dorene had her number, too. Should we go? Maybe Kurt would be there and several of his buddies. That would at least make it interesting. Still the rumors about the goings-on worried us. Also Dorene hadn't been specific about the date.

When we discovered it is for the Valentine's dance that would require dress-up, we were truly intrigued. No one liked to "dress-up" more than Wendy, and no one looked better in her fine clothes and subtle make-up than me. I knew that and I wasn't bragging. I, without adornment, was an invitation for admiration, a visual feast, an object of desire. I really did think highly of myself in those days. I've learned a few things since then. Still my attractiveness had caused me plenty of trouble already and could easily cause me more. But that was "their" problem, not mine, I decided. They could make it my problem if I didn't keep my wits about me.

Of course, the party was at the Hintons. More out of curiosity than desire, Wendy and I attended. We wanted to probe the guests about the sudden demise of our favorite teacher. Most likely no one would mention the incident or even had it in mind after two months and the subject supposedly laid to rest. We believed some of the guests in this crowd knew something about the beating. Whether the attackers intended such dire consequences for their behavior was uncertain. But a case could be made.

Dorene greeted us and introduced us to several attendees that we didn't know, especially the males from Sterling that had become, apparently, a regular part of The Kin socializing. Then as an offer of condolence she asked me if I still thought about the biology teacher's death. "Too bad that bar fight he was in the night before he left town has tarnished his reputation."

Russell's injuries were not a concern of the autopsy so how would Dorene know about them? And where did the bar fight rumor come from? Did she realize what she just said? And was she implying that those injuries had something to do with his death? Somebody must be running scared, and she unwittingly just opened a Pandora's box.

"I didn't know about any bar fight," I said feigning any knowledge of Russell's wounds.

"Oh, yes, it was during the Packer game when Russell started cheering for the Bears."

"Really, that's the first we've heard about it," Wendy chimed in. "That changes things."

"What do you fucking mean?" Lonnie Pepper challenged as more of the guests gathered around.

"It adds another perspective on his death. To think that Russell was a Bears fan," she said to derail their thoughts.

"Oh, come on. The cops, after their investigation, announced that it was an accident," David Dorsey stated as if he was the authority on the case.

"I didn't say it wasn't," Wendy mumbled, not wanting to comment further. She had planted the agitating seed that might blossom into a conviction. Anyway, she and I had to pursue the origin of their tale. This was not a matter to discuss by phone. So the plan was back to Ruiz and Gregory to certify their statements and to discount the bar fight. Then to the Watering Hole to question the owner, Berendt Hofstedder. But for the time being, the party loomed, the rec room dance floor churned with eager youth. The pairs didn't part from one another, but rather bumped their bums and oozed into each other as in a mating dance.

Kurt took my hand and pulled me close, too close for comfort, as someone sang. I laughed and pushed him away, eager to keep him off me but trying not to offend. Then Lonnie bumped my butt and David pulled me in. He whispered, "You don't think it was an accident, do you?"

"Why do you say that?"

"Look, the man who saw the car go down said there were no other cars nearby."

"Do you think there might have been? I don't understand."

"I mean if you think someone was chasing him. There wasn't."

"That's good to know. But something caused a healthy young man to die from an aneurism, don't you think?"

"That can happen to anybody. Genetics maybe, or stress."

"Yes, stress, think about that. What could have caused that much stress?

"Could be his mother's fucking illness." Lonnie speculated.

"Except that his mother wasn't sick." Damn, I said too much.

"Of course she was. He was going home to take care of her."

The song ended and I moved away with Lonnie staring after me quizzically. "The principal said so on the fuckin' PA," he shouted after her.

Wendy pulled me aside and said, "I'm sure somebody spiked the punch and look at those two, Kurt and Dorene, making out like rabbits."

"Come on, you guys. Let's go to Sterling," Kiki Bender yelled. "Come on, Let's bounce."

Suddenly the dance space emptied as coats and hats flashed everywhere and the party moved outside to the cars and a pickup. Wendy and I watched as they piled into the vehicles. What was in Sterling?

The red and white streamers and balloons hung from the ceiling dance and fluttered with the breeze from the open door. Half empty platters of cookies and cupcakes with candy hearts embedded sat on the serving table, but the punch bowl was empty. "Come on, you two, there's plenty of room," someone yelled as the voice faded out the door. It was clear the two sophs wouldn't be missed, unless Dorene realized her plot had flopped. It was also clear that false rumors of a bar fight had spread throughout the student body. Tomorrow we two detectives would resume our dormant careers after a two month hiatus.

First to Lincoln Ruiz to confirm that he and Russell had watched the entire Packers game without incident and just a couple of beers and that he had dropped him off at his condo and hadn't stayed to see that he entered safely. He should have; he knew that now. And Principal Gregory recounted his visit to Russell the Monday after the incident confirming Russell's story that he had been attacked as he was unlocking his front door. Finally, Berendt Hofstedder at the Watering Hole knew of no altercation that took place during or after the NFL game on that Sunday. So who started the rumor and why?

On Monday the gossip spread that the Sterling party had been raided by the local police for disturbing the peace first and then for underage drinking in a grounded houseboat parked along the river. Apparently, it had been a place for amusement more than once, even in the cold. The partiers had constructed a bonfire of firewood stacked a few yards away that blazed its warmth as they danced around it like sprites. It wasn't a Hinton boat. The owner and wife spend their winters in Florida somewhere. The underage drinkers were released to their parents after interrogation and a warning. The eighteen year old buyers of the booze that included Dorene Hinton and Lonnie Pepper were cited for a court appearance where they would be fined and ordered to community service.

More to the story seeped out in whispers that most believed were true, especially since Marvin Coleman was there. He said he happened to be driving by on his way home from visiting a friend in Hudson when he saw the fire and the lights on in the boat house when he approached. He heard laughing and shouting so he went to investigate. Since he was a member of the city council, the police decided not to probe any further in spite of the disturbed down comforters in the bunk beds inside. That was a scene left only to the imagination. Kurt Buford and Corey Morissey had left before the police arrived.

"There was no bar fight," I told Dorene in the lunchroom on Wednesday after the our investigation was updated. "Where did you hear that?"

"Everyone knows about it," she sneered.

"Why would anyone make up that story?" Wendy questioned.

Dorene shrugged and walked away.

The police had determined Russell's death was an accident with no mention of his black eye and cut face. Were they hiding something? Did they not want to investigate further? Was someone pressuring them to leave it alone?

The science club continued to meet after Russell's death with Ruiz as the advisor, but the passion had subsided. More imminent concerns occupied our minds. The other members tried to liven the discussions and plans, but with much less energy. Tara Morrisey had arranged for a speaker from the Wabasha Raptor Center across the river to talk to the club about their work and the receding habitat for local and migratory fowl. Joshua Balfour brought a bald and a golden eagle with him to enhance his talk. Clearly, he said, climate change was having a negative effect on wildlife habitats. We took smart phone photos of these magnificent creatures.

For a few days club members rallied behind their cause with each taking responsibility for researching some aspect of pollution from waste disposal and air pollution to fossil fuel energy and inadequate local laws. Billy Olson explored the web for the effects of the lumbering industry and paper mills on the environment and discovered that fifty percent of the forests in Wisconsin were privately owned and needed to follow the Wisconsin guidelines for safe harvesting and disposal of waste products. Several $10,000 fines had recently been administered to unlicensed loggers for over cutting private forested areas followed by inadequate waste management. Paper mills in other parts of the country had also been fined for toxic emissions from smoke stacks that contributed to acid rain that pollutes the streams and lakes and thus contaminates fish and reduces oxygen levels. His investigation intrigued me and inspired my interest in the Buford Post local lumber company.

Under the guise of a biology class project, I arranged for an interview with William Buford to acknowledge the contribution this grand company had made and still did to the community. I prepared a list of questions to that effect: jobs created, lumber products supplied to the area and throughout the Upper Midwest, charitable contributions to service organizations, churches, library, community center, sports programs, and more. No doubt, the Buford Lumber Company and Millworks had been a vital force to the community and needed accolades for its accomplishments. At least that perspective was my cover.

So I entered his office on the hill north of Buford Post and upon invitation sat across from him in a comfortable, brown leather, overstuffed swivel chair and answered positively when he asked me about my family and how we were enjoying Buford Post. I was well aware of the role he played in town and state Republican politics and knew I had to play my cards very carefully, not only to get the information I wanted, but to prevent him from affirming his suspicion about my motives.

So I began by praising him for his charitable contributions and support for community services, then focused on his family history in the lumber and milling industry, patiently waiting for him to finish story after story, until I suspected I would never get to the questions I most wanted answered. I marveled at his family ingenuity and cohesiveness in maintaining the business for generations, then asked questions about the current lumber supply, the waste products, and pollution control, very carefully I thought, not, however without agitating Mr. Buford as he verbally danced around my questions with illusive answers, enough so that I was quite sure he was covering up some of his misdeeds. I thanked him for answering my questions and promised I would show him my report before turning it in or publishing it in the school newspaper. He seemed satisfied that he had avoided suspicion and smiled a cordial goodbye. That was my perspective.

While Buford was willing to entertain my questions and support my school project, he seemed suspicious of my real motivation. Certainly, he knew of my involvement with the liberals who were blaming industry for causing global warming, an initiative he felt was contrary to business interests simply because the members were reacting to the hoax that most of his conservative friends considered it to be. No doubt he thought my attempts to make life difficult for him would go for naught, because he was well protected by his political friends. That was what I thought he believed. And I wasn't opposed to writing a complimentary essay about him without innuendo. My ulterior motive would have to remain interior for the time being. Most important, during that interview I recognized his discomfort with some of my more probing questions.

Wendy and I chatted about my suspicions. We questioned together if we should make them known to Ruiz, since he had much to lose by getting involved in an investigation of a town celebrity. But we decided to talk to him about my hunches and let him determine how involved he would like to be. Upon learning of our detective plan, he warned us about the logistics difficulty i.e. for transportation to different cites some miles north where most of the trees are harvested and the sawmills and paper mills are located with which Buford might be involved illegally. Also I was only fifteen and had no authority to ask for compliance and might jeopardize other investigations. He thought we should report our suspicions to the police and let them handle it.

Neither Wendy nor I trusted the police after their lack of inquiry over Russell's "accident" as they called it, the fact that they didn't probe further into the facial cuts and black eye that were not caused by the accident. So the police were out of the question. We had to pursue the investigation on our own. It was entirely possible that the beating that Hayward Russell received had something to do with the Bufords. In any case, there was more reason to investigate.

So how would we go about it. My mother audited the books at the Buford plant so she could with discretion get names, accounts and figures from the financial records if she was willing to do so. My father was certainly on our side in supporting our climate change cause and also had his suspicions about Russell's strange death, but would he allow his daughter to play detective and would he be the transportation we needed for our investigation? But we were getting ahead of ourselves. We had no idea at that point if there was anything to investigate and where we should start. We had to get more information before we could even approach parents in the matter. But how?

In court Dorene Hinton and Lonnie Pepper were reprimanded and ordered to 25 hours of service to the Highway Department picking up rubbish along state route 35 and a $100 fine, pending. Dorene in her overshoes and down coat trudging along the highway shoulder with a pick and trash bag was an obvious duck out of water. Lonnie, on the other hand, seemed used to that kind of humiliation. In his case it was water off a duck's back. I wondered what other Dorene indiscretions deserved reprimand if not arrest. She seemed to be up to her downy feathers in questionable games.

For the time being the investigation slowed to a stop. We took Ruiz's advice, because we had no other option. We were a queen and a rook on the chessboard with no king to check, not yet. My mother was our only option. If we told her our suspicions from all the questions we needed answered and she thought they were valid, we might convince her to play a valuable role, not realizing that role would mean compromising her integrity. But before we asked her, she was laid off with the unsatisfactory explanation that business was slowing down. The most likely explanation, however, was that my interview had set off an alarm in Mr. Buford who had to have something to hide. Mom, in pondering her dismissal, told my father about her confusion. She hadn't seen the noticeable slow down that Buford cited.

This happened at the breakfast table in the alcove of windows that overlooks the leafing vineyard. It's a beautiful sight, not meant to harbor strife or discontent. Rather it held the promise of intoxicating aromas and even more anticipated dreams to come true in another season of possibilities. I loved looking down the rows that were mine to tend. I was so much a part of what our family was achieving together. My brother, John, smiled as he worked with the irrigation system. I saw him now walking the rows checking the mechanism to be sure all was in working order.

I overheard part of the discussion and decided to tell Mom about the interview. At first she was salty and blamed me for sticking my nose into matters I shouldn't. After all the Bufords had had a legit, profitable business for generations and who was I, her daughter, to raise unwarranted suspicions. Besides what I was asking her to do would be unethical. Her accusatory words interrupted my vision of the vineyard, when I discovered that my father, was not so quick to judge me. He soothed my mother with "You don't need that job anyway and besides I need you working with me on the farm. Furthermore, "What if she's right?" He said. "What if things have changed in the Buford ethics due to economic difficulties? What if, for example, Hayward Russell needed to be taught a lesson about meddling?"

As Mom listened to Dad's questions, her face regained its color and she calmed. The vineyard brightened in the sunlight. Dad had always had a calming effect on Mom. I'm gratified that Dad gave credence to my suspicions and ever so gently brought Mom around, even though she remained piqued at my request of her. She saw that just maybe my suspicions had merit. Just maybe something was rotten in the state of Buford.

IN EARLY MARCH The Buford/Camden Jacks earned their way to the sectional playoffs that they had won due to the athletic skills of Kurt Buford and supporting cast. The team was on its way to the Wisconsin State High School Basketball Tournament in Madison. The players were joined, of course, by an entourage of fans, the cheerleading squad and the pep band that included me and Wendy and others who could afford to go. School officials made the accommodations at the Springhill Suites west of the university, but sojourners had to pay for their lodging and transportation to the Kohl Center where the games were played. The band, cheerleaders and team were housed on separate floors but had access to each other via cell phone, elevator, and staircases. The team was under curfew by coach's demand to prevent distraction from their task, but the cheerleaders, band members and many of the Buford fans were not timid about wandering the building in search of amusement. The airways were filled with text messages. The Kin were located on the second flour, players on the fourth. Most of the Jacks' fans were on the second or third. It was Coleman who had made the arrangements before the playoffs began, so confident was he that the team would earn a state tournament berth. He was one of the town's chief boosters. I was not so sure of his motives.

Most of the parents and fans found accommodations in other motels in the area. Wendy and I stayed with the band member units. We wouldn't miss a good time for anything and our parents approved with the admonition that we use common sense. Since the Westins and the Sunbergs had become good friends, the two families enjoyed walking the University streets, poking around in the buildings of the many colleges and eating out at the recommended restaurants, that is, when they were not attending the tournament. I heard about their afternoon adventures much later after the upcoming tragic evening had had time to settle.

The game wasn't even close between the Jacks and the Middleton Mavericks who poured the ball through the hoop like rain drops. The game ended at Mavericks 82 to the Jacks 51. Seldom had the Mississippi River towns reached the tournament at all and rarely were they a match for the more wealthy and well-staffed teams of the Madison suburbs. Disappointing, yes, but still a great opportunity for an adventure away from home. Kurt Buford had put the town on the map. He was sure to get the player of the tournament award after scoring 23 points against the loss to the Mavericks and 27 against their consolation win over the Riverton Raiders.

According to my dad, who described the scene some days later, at 4 p.m. the dignitaries from Buford Post met at the Esquire Club for a late afternoon repast by invitation from the Westins and the Buford Post National Band as a thank you for their service to the community. Just the parents were invited. We kids had our own amusements to attend to before the tournament finals between Middleton and Sheboygan High Schools at 7 p.m. that evening. Donald and Marilyn Westin served as royalty at the door to greet the dignitaries as they arrived dressed as they seldom did in their celebratory finery. First to arrive, Dan and Maggie Sunberg, my parents, the newcomers to the community. They smiled and thanked their hosts for being included with the town elite. Then arrived William and Emily Buford, followed by Earl and Martha Hinton, Olaf and Kari Odegaard, and Marvin Coleman and his wife Madeleine. I had never seen his wife. I told you that their daughter, Milli, was a good actress in the school plays.

None of the church leaders were invited because that would mean five more people increasing the number to fifteen, an impossible group to gather at a table and hold a viable conversation. Three bottles of champagne sat in silver ice buckets upon the white linen-covered table with matching dinner napkins and silver, Waterford glassware and bouquet of spring irises, tulips, and jonquils.

The guests sat in arrangements by choice, which turned out to be those closest in perspective and friendship: Donald Westin at the end with his wife Marilu beside him facing Marvin Coleman at the other end, next to him on his left his wife, Madeleine and across from her, Maggie Sunberg and beside her her husband Dan and Bill Buford across from him and his wife Emily beside him, and beside her, Earl Hinton and his wife Martha, and across from them, Kari and Olaf Odegaard. So there were twelve. When all were seated and the waiter had popped the champagne corks and poured the bubbly into each glass, Don Westin rose and offered a toast to the good citizens of Buford Post and the good fortune to have such fine kids, who were good students and athletes. "A toast to all of you and many others who have made our community such a fine place to live. And special welcome to our newcomers, the Sunbergs, about to add another dimension to our tourist industry. Here's to the first successful year as vintners."

"Hear, hear," came unison cries from the guests as they nodded in approval.

"They have already become our good friends as I'm sure to many of you. They can't help their Swedish background," he chuckled and all taunted the Sunbergs with attempts at compliments in a Swedish accent that rose and fell like a seesaw. Such gracious welcoming that the Sunbergs, Westins, and Odegaards, no doubt, accepted even though not all present were as enthused as the banker. After all the Westins and Sunbergs had daughters who were a pair of agitators, not to the liking of the Bufords, Hintons, and Colemans. Hinton joked in a half sneer, "I hear the Norwegians build outhouses and rent the basement out to the Swedes." Everyone laughed, especially my parents, who gave permission for others not to take offense.

So here they were evenly divided in perspective as they prepared to dine on the good graces of the local bank, certainly a thank you, but also an attempt to mollify whatever differences might interfere with community affairs. The topics of discussion had to be carefully chosen, not to incite a testy exchange. That limited them to family vacations, travels, redecorating, the latest cars, a seemingly safe topic if the subject didn't turn to "foreign" vehicles and hybrids and electrics. Unfortunately, it did. Odegaard brightened as he slipped in that he had been researching Volvo electric trucks that can travel over 150 miles on a single charge, to which Hinton inserted caustically, "And where does the electricity come from and how do you dispose of the batteries? They think they can get rid of gas and oil, but they can't. Our economy depends on fossil fuels. Don't fool yourself." He pulled his face from the middle of the table and sat back in his chair.

Silence for a moment, before Westin put in that it'd be a slow transition and "won't happen til long after we're gone, so let's realize that and do what we can however we can."

"What do you mean, do what we can? Buford piped up. "Like your daughter and yours, Sunberg, stirring up the community to take sides on a topic for which there are no sides to take. Look, my family has been in lumber for generations and has created and maintained our town with its initiative and vision and doesn't need government to keep peeking into our books and resources everyday to make sure we don't add another bit of carbon dioxide to the atmosphere or strip it of another breath of oxygen by cutting down a tree. You wouldn't have a home without our lumber. None of us would, so leave well enough alone. Thank God for our kids. Most of them understand the situation better than some of us here." Hinton and Buford had had their say. The opposition left well enough alone and didn't mention the Obama Presidency, clearly not the president of half of the guests at the table.

The meal arrived, mostly steaks on one side of the table, mostly fish and salad on the other to complete the stereotype as Odegaard raised his glass and smiled "To all of us good friends in spite of our differences." Each acknowledged his words and tried on a well rehearsed smiles appropriate for such an occasion. Then all ate in silence.

During dessert Sunberg congratulated the Hintons on their expansion and modernizing of their dock and houseboat rental offering that certainly would create a few more jobs and tourists. Others agreed and chimed in with accolades. Westin added that the Odegaard Cheese factory had had a banner year producing over two million pounds of cheese and supporting 76 workers. Great job. Coleman was happy to report the remodeling success of the community center which now housed an exercise room and programs for the locals that would keep us all more fit and healthy. Someone mentioned the Watering Hole Sports Bar, managed by Berendt Hofstedder, that provided an opportunity for locals and nearby residents to spend afternoons and sometimes evenings watching the Badgers or Packers over free popcorn and peanuts and a special on beer and sandwiches. He might have been another invitee to the party.

When the party dissolved at six so that the attendees had time to find their seats for the tournament finals, the men shook hands and the women gave hugs and thanked the Westins for the nice party, then disappeared to their cars. The Westins and Sunbergs had seats together twenty rows from the floor near the east basket.

WENDY AND I, who had seats with them, didn't show up by game time. Kurt Buford's charming persuasion convinced us to join him and friends for a meet up at a civic park. Unfortunately, Dorene Hinton was there. I should have known, but too late.

The gathering included two guys from Riverton, acquaintances of Kurt and Lonnie Pepper with some connection to the Buford Lumber Co, and Tanner Mortenson, who played forward on the basketball team and also tooted trumpet in the band and was a great jazz player, and Jasmine Dorsey, whom I didn't know very well. One guy from Riverton, Josh Richards, had vodka, but no mixes. Sorry, not for me. Not for Wendy either or Kurt for that matter because he had to be on the basketball court to receive an award after the final game. By five o'clock after sunset the cold air forced us to cuddle up. Lonnie swarmed around me like a gorilla in heat. Kurt was occupied with Dorene, and the Riverton guy, Josh, cozied up to Wendy. Why did I get talked into these sprees and convince Wendy to join me. I should know better by now. Kurt toyed with me then played the real game with Dorene. "We're cold," I say, "Take us back to the gym." I knew our parents were anxiously awaiting our arrival. I should have called them, but it wasn't convenient.

Wendy pushed Josh away and climbed in the back of the truck. The others piled in, too, except for the driver, Josh's buddy. I didn't know his name. Wendy and I squeezed together and buried our faces in each other's jackets to keep the raw wind off.

"Okay, guys, get ready for a joy ride," Josh called back and the driver floored the accelerator. It was a joy ride all right, whipping around the curves along a lake. Suddenly, Wendy and I, hanging on to each other, were airborne. We came apart and I hit the ground and felt my left arm snap as I skidded on my face to a stop. The next thing I knew I was in the ER.

Parents don't expect their teenage daughters to be late. By half time and Middleton leading 26 to 21 we were still not there. The men were uneasy, but the women were concerned. Marilyn Westin and Mom excused themselves with a "We'll be right back," and disappeared up the aisle to the entrance and box offices. Both tried calling their daughters without results.

Two policemen argued with each other and with what appeared to be a tournament official as the two women hurried toward them by the front entrance. "Our two daughters are missing," my mom blurted at one of the men, all three of which turned toward them. One of the policemen, the tallest, raised his hand as if to reassure them all, "Don't worry everything is under control."

"What do you mean?" She yelled, reddened with fear.

"There's been an accident just two blocks from this arena and several young people are in the hospital. We don't think anyone is badly hurt. A pickup truck with several kids in the back veered to avoid a school bus that was arriving to board students after the game. The sudden turn threw the kids in the open bed from the truck several yards. Luckily, no oncoming traffic struck them, but there were injuries."

"Who are the kids? Mom was shaking.

They were from a Mississippi River town and Riverton up north.

"Where's the hospital?"

"Down the road on Campus St."

The two women called their husbands, met them at their car in the ramp parking lot and sped to the hospital. They discovered that I had multiple bruises and a broken arm while Wendy was treated in ER with a badly bruised face. One young man, Tanner Mortenson was unconscious in ICU in serious condition. One of the passengers told the attendants that Tanner hit a light pole. The driver and passenger inside were treated for minor injuries and released to the police who held them in custody.

My dad, in an agitated and fearful state, prodded me for an explanation, but I was crying, unable to speak, and turned away. "Let her be, Dan," his wife calmed herself realizing her daughter would survive. "A broken arm will heal. She'll be all right." They let me rest.

Then the word spread that Tanner Mortenson had died of traumatic brain injury. Others had arrived including parents of the others in the accident, each questioning and probing, some in tears, others shaking in fear of what happened and what might have happened. The Mortensons were swimming in an ocean of disbelief.

"How could this happen? What were those kids doing in the back of a pickup in the frosty air? What were they thinking?" Dad mumbled inaudibly to Mom.

My arm hung uncomfortably cradled in a sling supporting a forearm cast. Ready now to leave the ER, I waited for Dad to drive up to fetch me and Mom home. He told me Tanner Mortenson had died.

"Did you know him?"

"Yes, he played trumpet in the band. My God, he died? Are the others okay?" I tried to tell them what happened to me. "Suddenly I feel like I'm on a roller coaster or inside a cement mixer and then I'm sliding on the grass and feel my arm snap. My God, Tanner? Yes, I know him. He's a good guy. He plays trumpet, hangs around with Kurt mostly and other band kids. You know he plays forward on the team."

"What were you doing in the pickup?"

"Well…" I searched for the words to tell them both. I told them the truth and included my stupid infatuation with Kurt that got us into this mess. "Please believe me when I tell you that neither Wendy nor I drank any of the vodka. Kurt didn't either, because he had to be on the basketball court for the awards after the final game. All I know is that Kurt and Tanner, Wendy and I and Jasmine were riding in the open bed of the pickup while this kid from Riverton, Josh Richards' friend, took us for a joy ride. Then bang. Oh, my God, how's Wendy? Is she okay?"

"Yes," my mother consoled. "She's all right, just bruised and scratched a bit but nothing broken."

"After checking out of the hospital, the driver and those with liquor on their breath were taken to the police station for interrogation. Thank God you weren't drinking."

"What were you doing with those kids?" Dad, still perplexed, demanded in dismay.

"I don't know why Wendy and I joined them. We don't even like Dorene. I thought we'd be safe with Kurt. It was so cold. And now Tanner's dead."

"Driving under the influence. It's amazing all of you weren't killed," Dad sighed in disbelief.

SUNDAY IS THE Lord's Day for many, but not for the Mortensons, not this Sunday. They didn't appear in church to hear Pastor Peters relate the grim news of the tragic death of one of the town's most promising young men. The congregation was visibly distraught. The sermon was more like a eulogy after which the pastor asked for a moment of silence and prayer. Dad and Mom, who allowed me to convalesce at home, tried to describe what happened. Slowly, methodically, the congregants walked into the cool sunshine that seemed not to warm them. Then the vacant church sat alone, empty and meaningless. Only Pastor Peters remained on the church steps overlooking his departing congregation dragging with them many unanswered questions.

I sat on my bed studying the teal, jade head feathers and orange beak of the mallard ducks quilted on my bedspread. The Sunday sun streamed in through the lacy white window curtains to spotlight the images. Tanner. I remembered him trying to avoid Rosy, who was all over him last fall on the houseboat, and he telling me that he talked with Kurt about it. They were real buddies, Kurt and Tanner. What must Kurt be feeling? I felt sorry for him but angry at him, too.

I wanted to scream at him but more I wanted to console him, talk to him, let him know that I cared. Tanner should not have died. He was going to Lawrence in the fall to study psychology, I thought. It didn't matter now. I didn't know what was happening. First, Russell and now Tanner, both declared accidents, but what kind of accidents. Those bedspread ducks weren't going to tell me. I had to talk to Kurt. Damn, my arm hurt. I had to see Wendy and make sure she was okay, but I didn't feel like going anywhere right then, and I didn't text her. I couldn't feel anything at all, just numb, numb, nothing. I leaned toward the pillow. A sharp pain shot up my arm. I could have died.

It was dark when I found myself upon the bedspread among those stupid ducks. The darkness was the most real substance in the room. I saw what was visible in a dark blur as if I looked into a well and watched the water rippling back at my half-bandaged face. I conjured up recent memories of Wendy and I playing detective as we sashayed through the lives of The Kin, and then to Kurt Buford and how he lured us into the after game revelry in the park and the subsequent truck ride with the two guys from Riverton who Kurt knew somehow. That was never explained but should have been. I needed Mom.

The alarm clock radio on my night stand read 10:30. My parents were, no doubt, in bed. I'd have to suffer the night, but not there swimming with these ducks. I got up but didn't turn on the light. I straightened the red and white school colors dress I'd been wearing all day, felt it relax back into place, found my cross training shoes on the floor beside me, sat in the puffed starry chair I had flopped into so often and tied on my shoes. I had to go somewhere.

I struggled to put my good arm through the sleeve of my rose down jacket. The casted arm wouldn't fit into the sleeve, so it hung inside my jacket. Quietly I avoided the creaks in the stairway, stepped out the door and crossed the road to the walking path. I wandered in the cool night air under the stars that disappeared as I passed under a street lamp, then brightened again in the darkness beyond. At the end of the path I continued down the hill and finally to the door of Lucy's Bar and Grill. I realized I still had the bandage on my face. Not much happening on a Sunday night, not enough to arouse a notice among the two barflies. The tables were mostly empty. The dark walnut stained booths sat like open boxes against the wall. I dropped onto one closest to the back wall, leaned back and closed my eyes.

A stocky elderly man stood over me and studied me quizzically. "What happened to your face? Sorry for asking. You can't be in here. You're under age." Then he recognized me. "Hey, I know you. You're the new winery kid, the Sundberg place on the hill. How'd you get here?"

"I walked."

"Christ, in the dark? By yourself? You crazy girl? Do your parents know you're here?"

"No," I hadn't thought about my parents. "I didn't know I was coming here. I just walked and here I am." I tried to smile but it came out as a frown. I unzipped my jacket to reveal my cast.

"What happened to your arm?"

"I've had a bad weekend."

"I guess you have. I'm calling your parents. What's your phone number?" He waited. "Never mind I'll look it up."

"It's only a mile or so," I said.

He walked behind the bar to get the phone number then pressed in the numbers on his iPhone.

I couldn't hear his words exactly, except for "you better come and get her" and something about her puffy eyes.

"Here's a cup of hot chocolate. Your father will be here in a few minutes. Do you want to talk?"

I just looked at him bewildered. "What about?"

"I just think you look like you need to talk."

I looked at him trying to understand his words as if he were inquiring the way to Milwaukee. He didn't make any sense.

"I'm sorry, no offense." He turned and walked away a bit perplexed.

I smiled, actually smiled, and called after him. "Thank you."

He shrugged his shoulders and put some glasses back on the shelf.

Dad and Mom burst in as Lucy, the owner, stood over me, whispering some kind words. I cowered in the corner of the booth, not to avoid abuse but to hide my shame. "I'm so sorry," I mumbled as my father slid in beside me, then pulled me out and to my feet. My mother threw her arms around me while I whimpered into her ear.

"We're sorry. We thought you were all right when you asked for alone time. We should have known you weren't." She petted my hair as she muttered through her tears, "Let's go home."

As we moves toward the door, my dad thanked the waiter and Lucy for their kindness to which Lucy nodded and the elder gentleman paused, speechless. My father explained, "She was in a car accident, broke her arm. One of her friends was killed."

Back at home we sat in the living room in two overstuffed chairs facing each other.

"You need to talk to us. Tell us how we can help." My father searched for words while my mom sat cramped beside me rubbing my back.

"That Riverton kid tried to hit on me. He tried to hit on me." I was in tears now, angry at him and angry at me for attracting every guy who came along. "Remember, Daddy, how you would tell me the story of the three little pigs and you always said, "You're house is made of bricks. If any guy tries to blow it down, he'll end up in a pot of boiling water. Right? And then you'd read me, *Good Night, Moon.*

"And I said, "Yes, Daddy. And I still say, Yes, Daddy. No one will blow my house down." I was still crying. I thought about the guys who had tried to blow my house down, and then Kurt for whom I considered opening the door, then bolting it shut. He was not to be trusted. I came to myself. "I can't believe Tanner died. Why was nobody else hurt seriously. I mean, what's a few scrapes and bruises and a broken arm." I said it, but it hurt.

"Let's not try to understand it now, dear. Who knows why things happen?" she cooed as she hugged me. "We love you, Libby," We'll help you. So will Pastor Peters."

"Not Pastor Peters, please. Just hold me." I didn't know why she mentioned him. We never went to church. They held me, both of them, all of us trying to be strong.

"Is there anything more you can tell us about what went on, the drinking, the conversation, anything?" Dad asked putting his hand up to prevent his wife's interference.

I thought a moment, then said, "Kurt said he would see him, Josh, in a few weeks when their dads would seal the deal. I thought, What deal, but didn't think anything more of it. Now I'd really like to know."

"Me, too," Libby, "Me, too. And I'm going to find out," Dad muttered.

"What will happen to the driver?"

"He'll be prosecuted, I'm sure. It's a serious offense that can get him years in prison. How old is he?"

"I don't know."

"That can make a difference, too. I hope he gets what he deserves, but I feel sorry for him, too. His stupidity caused a young man's death and has changed the direction of his own life."

I WAS EAGER to see Wendy in school the next morning. Before she arrived in first hour social studies class, Billy Olson stood before me his eyes full of concern. He was my height, slim, tawny, strong, though not athletic and not much interested in physical games, but very interested in the sciences and human rights. His father worked as a supervisor for the Odegaards and his mother was a needle worker and volunteer at the Community Center where she met and enjoyed the company of Sonny MaCray and his photos. Billy was a good guy, full of humor and good cheer and ready to share with me whatever I was feeling. More than anything he wanted to share his rich mind and curiosity with my passion for the planet and all living things. He said he expected me to be a doctor or a veterinarian or an ornithologist or ecologist, all professions that interest him, the subjects of which we could share if I would get over my infatuation for Kurt Buford. That Billy. Here he was standing in front of me not saying a word, but nodding as if he knew what I was feeling. I hardly realized that before. He knew me. "What happened to you?" He inquired hesitantly studying my face and arm.

I smiled at him and touch his shoulder. He nodded and we took our seats two rows apart. I couldn't help but look at him as he opened his social studies text and skimmed through some pages. I realized how pleased I was that he greeted me inside the classroom and for his concern.

Wendy arrived. I hugged her then stepped back to look at her face. I needed to know she was not angry with me for urging her to join the partying group. I apologized for not calling her the night before. She apologized, too.

"I should have called you right away."

"I'm fine," she said, "but look at me. I look like I've been thrown from a truck."

"Ya, well that's what happened."

"How's your arm?"

"It'll be okay. It was a clean break the doctor says so it should heal fine."

"Are you going to Tanner's funeral on Saturday?" Wendy asked.

"I suppose so. Are you?"

"Yes, you knew him better than I. Tell me about him. I know he was planning on Lawrence College in the fall."

"That's true. He had a fine mind. I don't know why he joined that party any more than why we did."

"I'm so sorry I got you into it."

"I'm not blaming you. You're my best friend and always will be." We hugged each other as if the hug would make all bad things go away.

"What's going to happen to the Riverton guys and Dorene and Lonnie and Jasmine? They were all drinking," she asked.

"They could go to jail for driving under the influence and causing Tanner's death. They won't be at the funeral. You can depend on that."

"What about Kurt?"

"He'll be there.

Billy had been listening to this entire conversation and shook his head in dismay. He searched for appropriate words, but found none except "I'm glad you're all right," and wondered if our decisions left him out of our company.

Kurt was there, at the funeral, sitting in the last pew, not to be conspicuous, not in position to say a few words on behalf of his friend. If anyone should, it should have been Kurt. But no, Kurt said nothing. Only Tanner's sister, Marci, and his friends, Corey and Terry Alden said a few words, mostly about friendship.

Wendy whispered to me as we sat quietly in the a middle pew in the Lutheran church, "I didn't know Tanner was friends with Corey,"

"Look, there's Rosy Masters. Remember her with Tanner at that houseboat party?

"Yes, but he didn't want anything to do with her."

"Didn't you know that they were dating?"

"Why wasn't she at the tournament?"

"Maybe she was sick."

"Maybe," Wendy commented unconvinced.

"She's in tears. This must be awful for her."

"I think she needs a friend."

A COUPLE OF days after Easter my dad told the story about his talk with Sonny MaCray. He worked at Lucy's. He was the guy who comforted me on my night sojourn at Lucy's Bar and Grill. A humble man of perhaps sixty, too young to retire and too old to seek his fortune, he helped Lucy out during the winter months until the fishing and boating season approached in mid April when he took care of the fishing boat and houseboat rental for the Hintons. Still of hardy musculature and stamina, he made repairs, filled the gas tanks of the outboard motors and painted the cabins and hulls as needed.

What he enjoyed most, however, was photography. With his mega pixel Canon zoom lens camera, he could capture the subtlest nuances of the river, its reflection of trees and clouds, nesting hawks, flying eagles and leaping bass on a line. Several of his photographs hung on the wall of the Community Center.

When my parents stopped in for lunch at Lucy's, he waited on them. As he took their order, Dad observed that he fidgeted uncomfortably as if he had something on his mind. They ordered salads and bagels.

"I knew Hayward Russell, the teacher," he said. Then he turned toward the kitchen.

When Sonny returned, Dad inquired tactfully, "Do you have something to tell us."

"Well, it's just that I know your daughter thought the world of him and rightly so. He was a good man and I'm sure he was a good teacher. I live in the building across the street from his condo. He enjoyed my photographs. He loved nature and the river.

He liked to take a boat out and float in the backwaters. Didn't fish. Just mused, I think. Great guy."

Neither of my parents spoke except to nod in agreement.

"I have photos." He looked at them in earnest. "I saw two guys jump him. It was dark, but I have their images from the street lamp down the block. I don't know them, but I have the photos."

"My God. Did they say anything?"

"I heard one of the guys say, 'You fucking troublemaker."

"Why haven't you turned the photos over to the police."

He hung his head. "I don't know. I wish I had. I don't like trouble."

"Can we see them?"

"Yes, they're in my apartment. Come over this evening after seven."

"Thank you. We'll be there."

My parents could hardly finish their meal, traumatized by the new information and speculating on what the photos might reveal.

They saw the photos as promised at Sonny's apartment half submerged below ground level with windows that opened for ventilation. In one window facing the street was an air conditioner. The other front window had an upward view across the street to the apartment complex where Hayward Russell lived. Sonny's photos were remarkably clear and sharp considering they were taken in poor light. One photo captured the face of one of attackers as he turned toward the street after the beating but too dark to discern features enough to identify him. Perhaps someone who knew him could. Maybe me. But should they bring me into this investigation? Why not, I was the first detective on the scene and now I had even more at stake. Perhaps the perpetrators had more at stake than silencing a passionate teacher. Sonny allowed my parents to take the photos with them to show me, but not to turn them over to the police.

Sonny had other concerns about some of the youth that rented houseboats from him. He had little regard for Dorene Hinton and had had many occasions to witness her behavior and the way she commanded her girlfriends. "The Kin, she calls them, about five of them, under her control." He could tell them more if they wanted to hear.

"Maybe later, but for now let's focus on identifying the culprits in your photos,"

"I agree."

"Thank you for these." Dad held them up. Mom was about to hug him, but didn't, just smiled a thank you.

"I want Wendy and Billy to see the photos, too. He was as upset about Russell's death as we were. I want him part of our team." The three of us studied the dark photos while Dad and Mom watched us. Neither Billy nor Wendy could connect, but I recognized the one man.

"I know who he is," I blurted. I've seen him at parties. It's Lonnie Pepper. He was coming on to me at the Madison park. He graduated a couple of years ago and works for the Bufords. He's an skank\. When he's around Kurt Buford, he brings out the worst in him. I don't know why Kurt hangs out with him and Dorene. That bitch."

Mom put her hand on my shoulder, looked me in the eye and said deliberately, "You've been using too much of they kind of language, Libby. Please don't. It's so unbecoming."

Billy smirked, but said nothing. Clearly he agreed with my mom.

"Sorry, Mom, it's just that I get so angry and now Lonnie connects Kurt to what happened to our teacher. I just get so pissed. I have to say it, sorry."

"So now what?" Dad mused. "How do we prove that it was Lonnie and how do we find out about the other guy and why they did this? They probably didn't mean to kill him, but they injured him badly enough to cause his death on the road the next day."

"I'll talk to him like I'm interested in him," I sparked.

"No, you won't," Billy chimed in. "That could be dangerous and if he gets the idea that you know something that could incriminate him, he might act against you in a way that might be worse than a broken arm."

"I think Sonny MaCray might help when we tell him who the attacker was. He doesn't like that bunch and feels terrible about waiting so long to share his photos."

SONNY MACRAY DID help. He enticed Lonny Pepper to help him to prepare the houseboats for the upcoming season for a twelve dollar an hour wage, acceptable to Hinton. Lonny with his swagger was honored that Sonny would choose him, not suspecting an ulterior motive.

The next Saturday the two of them painted the outside of one of the three houseboats blue. The other two were slated for a coating of maroon and white.

"So who are you hanging out with these days, Lonnie?" Sonny inquired nonchalantly.

"Oh, you know, Corey Morissey's a damn good friend. We like to get into trouble together, if you fuckin' know what I mean." He laughed.

"Yeah, I fuckin' know what you mean," Sonny mimicked "a few beers, a couple of gals." He hit him on the shoulder with his free hand.

"I bet you were a real stud in your day."

"I wouldn't say that, but I had my moments."

"Yeah? You ever get fuckin' married?"

"Almost, but the woman I was going to love forever, decided on another guy. That was when I lived up near Brainard. I was farming then, but I wasn't good at it. I wanted to have more time to do what I like."

"What's that?"

"Taking photographs. Take a look at some of them hanging in the Community Center."

"Where do you live?"

"Right here in town."

"Where in town?"

"On Second Street, right across from where that teacher who died lived."

Yeah, what a fuckin' accident."

"It didn't seem like an accident to me."

"Really, why the fuck not?"

"It's a strange thing, but the night before he died I heard a commotion outside and I saw two guys pounding on him and then ran off. Hayward was able to unlock his door and get inside, so I thought he wasn't badly hurt. I should have gone over there to see if he was all right, but I didn't. I didn't want to get involved in whatever that was about."

"Yeah, good for you. Not a fuckin' good idea to get involved in some fuckin' dark off like that," he emphasized visibly shaken.

"So I let it go."

Lonnie was quiet, not sure what to make of this turn of events. Sonny, on the other hand, had another name for follow up— Corey Morissey. He had to find a way to get some information from him. First, reported to my dad.

That night at the kitchen table, the place where we most liked to talk, strange as it was because we had beautiful overstuffed chairs in the den facing the fireplace, Sonny told Dad, "Lonnie trembled when I told him I saw two guys beat up Hayward Russell. It's hard to be friendly with him. For him it's fuckin' this and fuckin' that. What a bore. He pretends to commiserate with me about Russell's loss, but I could see that he was working hard to protect himself. I'm convinced he was one of the two, and I'm guessing that his good friend Corey Morissey was the other. But why? Who put them up to it?" Sonny mused as he reported his conversation.

"That we have to find out," Dad commented.

I struggled to keep silent. I wanted so much to get Lonnie's confession even though a false move could be dangerous. I had a plan—Tara, Tara Morissey, Corey's sister. She had been quite active in the science club and disapproved of her brother's associates, especially his friend, Lonnie Pepper.

"That loser," Tara grimaces, as she sat across from me in the lunchroom on Tuesday the next week. "Whenever he's at our place with Corey, he hits on me and Corey just laughs. What a deadbeat."

Still she was protective of her brother. She loved him in spite of the crowd he ran with. She told him how worried she was about him, but he put her down as a "prissy miss." Whenever she chided him, that's what he said, "prissy miss," and laughed at her. She was afraid he'd get into real trouble with those guys and especially Dorene who kept Kurt salivating. "She's the worst."

I felt sorry for her to have a brother she couldn't admire. He had always looked out for her as they were growing up. Teasing and taunting her, yes, but always in fun. She knew he would never let Lonnie or anybody take advantage of her, even though she wasn't sure that he would be protective of other girls. She suspected he had been "too involved" in more than one of their parties. As for him, he didn't approve of her activities with the Science Club and that global warming nonsense. That bothered her, too. She wanted him to understand the urgency of fighting climate change, but it was not to be.

"Are you sure there were only two assailants attacking Russell?" I asked when I made a special trip to Lucy's to talk with Sonny.

"I saw only two beating on him, but they ran down the street to a getaway car. I couldn't get a license number or even the model of the car except that it was a hatchback of some kind, I think. No, I don't even know that for sure."

"So three were involved."

"Yeah, I guess that's right."

"Who might be the third?"

"I have no idea. Well, maybe I do. But I'd rather not say at this point. I don't want to jump to conclusions."

"I understand. That's for us to find out."

"It must feel good to have your cast off," he smiled.

"Yes, what a bother and a constant itch? I had to use a chopstick to poke under the cast to scratch."

"I can see the marks," he laughed.

"But I can't get the itch out of my brain."

"Be careful."

I nodded.

So I had more to extract from Tara, who seemed willing to speak her mind but not if it implicated her brother. This time we talked in the vacant auditorium facing the stage.

"Who besides Lonnie does Corey hang out with, if you don't mind my asking."

"Of course not. It's Kurt, you know, Kurt Buford."

"Yeah, I know."

"So what do they do together?"

"I have no fucking idea." Coarse language for her.

That's the end of that conversation since Tara became more irritated as she spoke. She hated that twosome and threesome because they always seemed to get into trouble.

PART TWO

In Sun and Rain

We Sunbergs called a hiatus to the spring vintner activities and accepted an Anderson invitation to their cabin on Memorial Weekend. Upon my invitation, Wendy agreed to come. John, my older brother, stayed home to take care of some things that vintners do to nurture the vines.

The open windows allowed the spring aromas in on this gloriously warm late May day. Dad's Prius hummed to the tune of Norah Jones, "Come on home and turn me on." Wavy, but I buttoned Pandora track, Gotye, "Someone I Used to Know," that was really lit. I, with permit placed conveniently in the glove compartment, drove with Dad, the navigator, in the passenger seat and Mom and Wendy in the back seat peering at the passing landscape hoping to God that I would stay on the road. The morning sun stuttering through the red pines of northern Wisconsin could send an epileptic into fits, but to these travelers it seemed like a flip book movie with the added scent of pine needles. We cruised the two lane road over rolling hills past forests of aspen and birch and more pines toward our destination. Wendy fiddled with her phone.

Before the last few miles I, with my father's input, drove into Riverton to choose the groceries at Cub for the Anderson table. There at the check out counter was Marvin Coleman from Buford Post. Not to be seen, Dad motioned to us to stand with him in the first aisle. We said nothing, just watched as Coleman paid for a few scant items and disappeared out the door. Dad hurried to the window to follow him to his vehicle. I sneaked up behind him, so did Mom. "Dorene Hinton." Wendy whispered. "Oh, my God, Oh, my God." I breathed. "Dorene is in the passenger seat." We purchased the hamburger and buns, baked beans, a chocolate cheese cake, two bottles of Wisconsin wine from Seven Hawks Vineyard, potato chips and enough greens for a Caesar salad, and oh, yes, a dozen eggs and bacon. Not a vegetarian among us but some discussion of the possibility some day in the future.

During happy hour Dad asked Roy if he was familiar with the Richards. "Of course. They own the largest private forest in northern Wisconsin, nearly 10,000 acres, surrounding their own private lake. They have controlling interest in the paper mill and supply lumber to several mills. Why do you ask?"

Not ready to answer that question, he asked another. "Do you know Marvin Coleman?"

"I don't know him, but I know of him. He apparently works for a lumber company and comes here from time to time. I guess he has business with the Richards."

"Well, let's enjoy our dinner," Dad turned the conversation.

So that ended it for the moment, but I knew Dad was stewing about something, some plan maybe. He knew of the Richards only because of me and the terrible accident that caused Tanner's death.

This time it wasn't me that took the initiative, but rather my dad who had remained suspicious ever since the dinner gathering sponsored by the Westins in Madison during the basketball tournament. The conversation at that event caused him to believe that Hayward Russell's beating and subsequent death hung in the air over the attendees. He surmised that somebody there knew something about it. Then too my speculations about the Richards had peaked his interest. He was curious about the Buford/Riverton connection brought to light by the irresponsible ride that killed Tanner Mortenson and about Kurt Buford's association with Josh Richards.

That evening when Maia, the Anderson daughter, Wendy and I were supposed to be in bed, I climbed down from the loft to get a Mello Yellow from the kitchen refrigerator. I heard Dad and Anderson talking and I listened. Dad pointed out what he and Mom saw at Cub, that Dorene was the girlfriend of Kurt Buford, and that Coleman, a Buford Post councilman, had been seen at an unseemly party in Sterling, and then the accident from the pickup.

"Something is going on that we should know."

"Holy Crap," Roy muttered.

"Do you know where the Richards property is?" Dad asked.

"Yeah, I know where the entrance to their estate is."

"Are there any back roads and entrances?"

"I don't know, but we could explore. What do you hope to find?"

"I'm not sure, but I have a hunch."

They let their wives know, but excluded Wendy, me and Maia from the intriguing information. They planned an early morning search under the guise of going out for morning coffee at Starbucks, just men talk.

I didn't buy it. Those two were up to something and I wanted in. After all, we were the detectives, me and Wendy.

They drove Roy's Subaru Legacy Outback to avoid recognition. The three of us followed in the Prius, Wendy driving because she had her license. After three or four miles of winding roads through pines that clung to the two lane blacktop, a few birches poked through the brief openings. The two men passed an ornate iron gate with woven iron letters spelling out Richards. Masoned brick posts supported the seeing eye gate that allowed for an interesting view of the roadway to a brick two story mansion and several log cabins that faded into the forest. They continued on with only a slight deceleration hoping to find a route around the grounds. No luck. Roy u-turned to pass by once more and looked for a route the other way around. We saw them coming in time to drive into a lane under tree cover. This time luck smiled on them, not another entry but a break in the fence where apparently a back entrance had been. We waited a few minutes then followed. Up ahead we saw the Subaru parked along the roadway and stopped,

"What do we do?" Wendy asked.

"We tail them."

"What if they see us?"

"We'll take that chance."

"I'm scared." Maia trembled.

"You can wait here if you want."

"No, I'll come."

The overgrowth had nearly erased any attempt to enter, but on foot we could break through. We heard them up ahead and kept our distance. Rusted barbed wire lay on the ground threatening injury. Nettles blocked our passageway as if standing guard. Unfortunately, we were clothed in our shorts and sandals. We passed, in spite of the discomfort the itch weed caused, shielding our bare arms and legs as we swished by after which the forest floor opened under the trees to a pine needle floor that offered no path but many options in any direction. We didn't have a compass and couldn't tell which way they might have turned. We waited, listened and hoped to God we didn't get lost. We had to rely on the sun through the trees to keep our bearings and find our way back to the Prius.

After some distance walking as straight ahead as we could, we came to an opening where acres of trees, all pine, had been recently cut, most of which had been hauled away, but some lay yet to be transported. We didn't dare cross that open space in fear of being detected. Neither Wendy nor I had any knowledge of what was legal or illegal cutting of timber, but we knew what we saw.

"Maybe we better go back," Wendy said.

"Yes, we should go back," Maia agreed.

To walk around the area would take too long and an easy way to get lost, so we had to give it up. We were back at the Andersons well before Dad and Roy arrived and did what we could to release the itching without alerting Mom. We tried desperately to keep from scratching.

"You didn't really go to Starbucks for coffee this morning, did you." I confronted Dad at lunch time.

"Why do you say that?" Dad responded.

"For one thing your arms are scratched and red from walking through something and for another, after you thought I had gone to bed I heard you from the kitchen say to Roy that you two should explore the Richards place. What's that all about?" I had put on my blue jeans to hide the obvious inflammations.

"Well, we'll tell you now, so if you're ready to listen without interruption, I'll ask Roy to join us."

"I'll get Wendy and Maia."

"Why Maia?" Roy questioned startled.

When the five of us sat at the kitchen table chewing on hotdogs and potato salad, Dad inquired, "Wendy, how did you get those scratches on your arms?"

"Oh, I don't know." Wendy strained for an explanation.

"It must have been when you slipped off the dock this morning," I put in.

Wendy wouldn't talk.

"You followed us, didn't you?" Dad accused.

"Well, yes, we did because it isn't fair that you exclude us from the investigation. We're part of this, you know."

"Look, we didn't include you because it could be dangerous."
Roy tried to console.

I was angry, but didn't go off in a huff because I had to find
out what they saw.

"Okay, that's done, but you have to tell us all." I said glaring
at him.

"That's fair. First, Libby, I need to know if you remember
anything more what Kurt Buford and Josh Richards said to each
other on the night of the accident. Anything about up north
or their parents relationship or anybody else that visited the
Richards, anything."

"Just that Josh expected to see Kurt soon and to bring Dorene."

"He said that, "Bring Dorene?"

"Yes, and any of their other friends."

"So how far did you follow us?"

"We stopped at the clearing.

"You better put some anti-itch cream on your arms. You're
going to scratch yourself raw," Roy chuckled. "Maia had on long
pants at least."

Dad continued, "So after the clear cut area, we continued
on through the open area where we came upon machinery and
trucks silently parked for the holiday weekend. Among them sat
a bull dozer, a backhoe, a tractor with trailer behind obviously
to haul lumber cut to size. The clearing went on forever among
cut logs and stumps yet to be removed by backhoe in preparation
for plowing and replanting. That's what we believe. Right, Roy?"
He nodded. "At the clearing's end, once more we wound our way
toward an uncertain destination looking in earnest for some sign
of life, a building at least that might indicate our proximity to
the Richards estate. Suddenly we came upon a row of blossoming
lilac bushes with aroma so pleasant we stopped to inhale while
speculating what we would find on the other side, then pushed
through. Ahead, maybe thirty yards was a circular driveway

supporting three automobiles, one having just arrived with two passengers about to emerge from the Ford Fusion. Kurt Buford showed his head first on the far side as Lonnie Pepper pushed the door open closest to them. We huddled back among the lilac leaves to avoid detection. Kurt and Lonnie, there at the Richards. I tried to remember what you said about Kurt and the guy who drove the pickup the night of the accident. Maybe you know more than you told me. In whispers Roy and I discussed whether we should talk with you and I told Roy about Coleman and Dorene Hinton. We didn't want to be detected so we waited for them to go inside the house, then high tailed it through the cut carnage and forest growth that blocked our way. We found the Subaru and here we are.

"I think their weekend party is just beginning and more guests will arrive soon, more guests, mostly female, probably Dorene's friends," Dad continued.

"The Kin," I said.

"So you think this party leaves something to be desired?" Roy commented.

"Oh, there's plenty to be desired." I quipped.

"What's the Kin?" He asked.

No one responded.

"I saw Coleman at the houseboat party in February," I said, "It didn't make sense that he was there. I don't know what to think."

"Let's not come to hasty conclusions. It may be an innocent gathering of friends," Roy commented, trying to keep our imaginations from overflowing. "They have quite a spread in the middle of the forest built on their own lake."

"Yeah, sure." Dad mused, then brightened. "Let's help Roy put the dock in and get the boats out. It's too nice a day to be dwelling on this stuff, whatever stuff it is."

THE ANDERSONS HAVE a floating dock that rolls out section by section on attachable barrels that supposedly prevent the installers from immersing themselves in the cold water. Supposedly, because it never happened that way. The barrel tubes often jammed and wouldn't release so someone had to get in the water to make the adjustment. Once in and numb and breathing again, the unfortunate participant shivered through the procedure, and sloshed his way back to shore eager for several towels of warmth.

When the dock was in, Roy pulled the pontoon boat from the boathouse and backed it into the lake followed by the Lund fishing boat and two kayaks that Wendy and I carried to the water front. That afternoon and Sunday and most of the day Monday offered pontoon lounging and happy hour with Wisconsin Cheeses from Odegaards and wines from Seven Hawks and lots of conversation about the new vineyard adventure that excited us all. Dad and Mom bubbled with enthusiasm over their accomplishments, boasting about their competence and efficiency, praising son John for his energy and skill installing the irrigation system and my after school assistance in planting. This teamwork made it possible for this weekend's escape to Camp Anderson, as we called it, although no one had to camp out. The cabin has three bedrooms and a loft but after the first night we put up a three man Eureka tent for the three of us to breathe in the night air and girl talk. No forecast of rain.

When Monday afternoon demanded pack up time, we said our goodbyes and drove a quiet three hours back to Buford Post. Quiet, except for the hum of the Prius. After a disturbing beginning of the weekend that slipped naturally into water activities and catch-up conversation, we relaxed to the murmur of the road, so pleasant that all concerns evaporated into the spring air. That contentment stayed with us all the way home. Still we had our own musings not to be shared at that moment, personal musings, all mine kind of musings. As we pulled into the parking space in front of our house, those musings turned to the matters at hand, tomorrow, for example, and unsettled matters, particularly for me and I suspected my dad who needed to probe the Richards company. Dad wouldn't let that go and neither would I.

In the next few days he proceeded with a plan. First, it was to confer with Sonny again about his boss, Earl Hinton. What he wanted to know bubbled up slowly as if from a spring. What did Hinton think of his daughter, Dorene, for whom Sonny had so little respect. Once more Dad and I found Sonny at Lucy's Bar and Grill to probe his mind. We wanted him to give us any facts about Dorene from his observation, and we wondered if he had had any conversations with Hinton about her. "What I know is strictly hear say. You know as much as I do except that she loves to hang around the guests on the boat dock in her bikini strutting her stuff, and she has stuff to strut."

He said that Hinton was either completely oblivious of his daughter's activities, or passed them off as teen behavior of little consequence. As far as Sonny knew, Hinton had never chastised his daughter for her misdeeds. Even after the drinking, disturbing the peace party, her minor community service sentence, and her drunken ride in the pickup in Madison, he shrugged it off as teenagers having a little fun that sometimes goes horribly wrong. "Accidents happen," Hinton said.

"Just wanted your perspective," Dad remarked. "I figured as such."

"Do you know if Marvin Coleman was involved in any of their events?"

"Coleman, the councilman? No, I don't. Was he?"

"I don't know either, but there is some evidence, I think."

"Really."

Dad didn't explain and Sonny didn't ask.

Part two of the plan focused on Earl Hinton himself. Since he and Earl were quite opposite in views, especially political, he had never had much conversation with the man. Still he believed him to be a loving father, who would protect his daughter's virtue. Only a tactful, non-threatening approach would allow for them to have a conversation about his daughter. Maybe her relationship with Kurt Buford or my casual acquaintance with her could be an opening. Maybe he could mention the unfortunate accident at the basketball tournamen or something about the Richards place up north.

Dad hadn't decided on his approach when we pulled into the Amoco station for a refill and stopped at the food mart for a snack. He loved the peanut butter filled pretzel squares. Hinton was restocking one bait bin with shiners, fat head minnows, and chubs and another with crappie minnows. Dad asked me to wait in the car to prevent Hinton from clamming up when he saw me, a climate change trouble maker. I agreed reluctantly, but realized he had a point. When Dad stepped into the back room he noticed new outboard Johnson and Mercury motors screwed onto supporting posts.

As he approached, Hinton swirls out a "Hey, Sunberg, how ya doin. Don't see you in here very often."

"No, I guess when I'm here for gas, you're at the dock or tending to a houseboat."

"Yeah, there's lots to do around here. Can hardly catch my breath. What a great Memorial weekend. Never nicer weather."

"Never. We were up north at the Anderson place on Boom Lake. I knew Anderson from South Dakota. Do you have a place up there somewhere?

"No, in summer I'm too busy here to take time off. You're lucky to have a friend to visit."

"You're right about that. I thought you might be up there because I saw your daughter at Cub supermarket, so I thought you might be around somewhere."

"You saw my daughter? Where?"

"In Riverton at the supermarket."

"There must be some mistake. My daughter was here in Buford Post. She had a date with Kurt Buford Saturday night."

"Maybe I was mistaken. It sure looked like her."

"Was she with anyone?"

"Well, yes, with Marvin Coleman."

Hinton scrubbed his hands as if trying to remove dried paint. His face reddened, his hands shook. He turned away as if to hide tears. But there were no tears above his clenched jaw.

"That Son of a Bitch."

"I'm sorry. I assumed you were up there with the Colemans, and she and Coleman were running some errands."

"Thanks. Mr Coleman has some explaining to do and so does my daughter.

"I'm really sorry. I hope everything is all right."

"I'll make it right. You can bet on it."

ON WEDNESDAY AFTER my last class Kurt waited for me in the hall and greeted me with an enthusiasm that set me back. He gushed how he couldn't get me out of his mind, how he was such a fool to spend his time with Dorene, who had the mind of a moth and the fidelity of a rabbit. He looked at me with such longing and told me how beautiful I was and to come with him right now to the Watering Hole to have a talk.

Startled, yet intrigued, I reminded him that I'm underage and can't enter a bar.

"It's okay if we just have cokes. They have free popcorn," he chuckled.

I agreed to go with him to assess him further based on my new information, so he shoved my bicycle in the back of his SUV. Little Miss Detective would have to keep her wits about her.

We ordered cokes, dished up two bowls of popcorn and settled into a booth that I had seen only once before when I came there to inquire about the supposed fight that Hayward Russell had over a football game. Sitting across from Kurt at this moment, I tried not to show discomfort knowing what I thought I knew about him. His sweet talk stirred my suspicions. He wanted something from me. I was afraid to think what.

I started the conversation before he had an opportunity to gush further.

"Did you have a nice time in Riverton?"

"How did you know I was there?" He inquired suspiciously.

"We were at Cub when we saw your SUV pass, you and Lonnie." Not exactly the truth, but believable.

"Yeah, we were up there for a weekend retreat with some of the guys and gals."

"Like Dorene?"

"Well, yeah, she was there but we had a falling out. She was getting it on with some guy."

"Sorry to hear that. That must have bruised your ego. Who was the guy?"

"We weren't getting along very well anyway and I realized I have feelings for you."

"Who was the guy?"

"I don't know, some guy."

"So I left and came home."

"Good for you."

"But listen. I want to spend some time with you. I'll be here most of the summer working for my dad before I go off to Madison in August. Let's hang out. What do you say?"

A bit flattered, but wary, intrigued and, I have to admit, stimulated, I agreed, sort of. I said, "What do you have in mind?"

He said he'd scoop me Friday night and we'd get a power boat at Hinton's and cruise the river.

"Just the two of us?"

"Just the two of us." He smiled an enigmatic smile that I decided not to interpret.

Then he enthused about the football program at U of W and that he'd be red-shirted his freshman year so he'd be eligible for five years, "so don't expect anything right away. They're grooming me for a starting quarterback my sophomore year." Then he took me home, unloaded my bike, gave me a hug and kissed me on the ear.

Friday evening it was just the two of us, as he said. He rented a Crest Liner power boat with a 75 hp motor and a canopy from Hinton who eyed us suspiciously. He must have seen me as a rival for his daughter. I guessed he wondered what Kurt Buford wanted with me. Then he smiled at Kurt and I thought I knew. Frankly, I was nervous, even afraid of what was in store for me. I almost decided not to go, but I couldn't say it. Soon we were out on the river watching the cruisers among the fishing boats and barges, then floating with the current. We watched the sun drop behind the Minnesota hills. He knew the river well enough to find a sandbar and dropped anchor. He sat beside me and pulled me against him to which I comply though still protective. I made it clear that his arms and hands were restricted to cuddling and that parts of my body were off limits. Reluctantly I admitted he felt good. I allowed my head to rest on his shoulder as we gently bobbed to the waves of each passing boat. He remained a gentleman. I didn't know what to think of him, but oh how I wanted him to be real, not the phony I suspected him to be. He might know the river, but he wasn't prepared for the mosquitoes. As the sun disappeared, they arrived like an insect army, complete with air force and dive bombers. These menaces ruined the beauty and romance in one minute. "Let's get out of here before we have no blood left," I moaned swatting as many as I could.

Hinton greeted us laughing. "I could have told you about the mosquitoes but I guessed you'd figure it out for yourselves.

"Thanks a lot," Kurt sneered.

At my door he kissed me, a real kiss, that I not only allowed it but participated in it fully. It was good, so good.

"Good night," he whispered.

"Good night."

"I'll dream of you."

I didn't respond but I'm thinking, "Me, too."

In bed pulling the covers around me, I chastised myself. Why was I letting this happen? I was as confused about me as I was about him.

No rain interfered with events for the next two weeks. Graduation night on Thursday June 9th was no exception. Whenever possible the ceremony was held on the football field with folding chairs lined up in several rows for the guests, first of whom were the parents, relatives and special friends of the graduates. We recognized Kurt Buford in red cap and gown, and further down the line, Dorene Hinton, and further on Rosy Masters and Jasmine Dorsey. I recognized Jasmine who was with us on the tragic ride and was a member of the Kin, and remembered that Rosy had an interest in Tanner. Principal Gregory announced the winners of scholarships and grants and high honors to the outstanding members of the senior class.

First, the valedictorian and salutatorian and local awards from the service clubs. Then he paused before he began his accolade of the most gifted athlete in the history of Buford Post. He stated his record breaking passes for touchdowns, his twenty-two point average on the basketball court, his twelve home runs for the baseball team, his full ride athletic scholarship to the University of Wisconsin football program, and best athlete of the state basketball tournament that he received in absentia due to the accident that took the life of one of our finest young men, Tanner Mortenson. Then he asked the attendees and graduates to share a moment of silence for our tragic loss. I wondered what Kurt was feeling at this moment. When that moment passed he asked Kurt to come to the podium to receive his award. His parents led the standing ovation. Truly, the community was excited, not only for this moment honoring a phenomenal young athlete, but for all the entertainment he had brought them with his spectacular plays and winning teams. The ovation went on. We, too, and the Westins who stood beside us, and the Odegaards a few rows to their left joined in a hardy applause. In spite of some controversies that we didn't want to believe, we were pleased to applaud this young man and to see the joy on his parents' faces. Then the handout of diplomas, not the real diploma, but the casing in which it would be when each student picked it up in the principal's office the day before the end of the school year.

Those in doubt of Kurt Buford's character left that celebration doubting themselves. It didn't seem possible that this young man could be involved in improper, or worse yet, criminal behavior. Perhaps we should leave well enough alone and let natural consequences take their course. Perhaps not. That was the dilemma. We, yes we, because each of us investigators in one way or another had such misgivings and I had to admit, if to no one else, he enthralled me. After pushing himself on me in the early days of our meeting, he had become a perfect gentleman, a bit to my regret. I remembered well his kiss. And now for the last two weeks we had been a couple. He was charming, no doubt about that. He intended that he and I would spend many summer days together and who knew what might happen if I allowed it.

As was the custom, the graduates were treated to an all night graduation party put on by the parents and financed by the local businesses. There were games, eats, bands from surrounding communities, dancing, and prizes, one of which was a drawing for a three year old Ford Escape offered by the Lacrosse dealership patronized by the Bufords and several others in the community. Most upsetting for me was that Dorene Hinton would be there, no doubt working her wiles on Kurt, who I hoped was impervious. I still wasn't sure if their relationship had ended.

I had guarded against his wiles, his well-schooled romancing. I spent time with him at my peril. I would not be another notch on his sword of conquests if that was what this courtship was about. How many dates before I succumbed? Was that his challenge? Or was he legit? Was he really interested in me? Did I deep down believe he was the kind of man I wanted? Soon he'd be at the U with all those college girls fawning over him. Would he remember me or would he sweet talk one or more of them as he was sweet talking me? I couldn't sleep thinking about it. His attempt at clarification of his brief stay up north, didn't ring true. I hoped it was. Then again, if his motives in this relationship were suspect, so were mine. I had to admit that I wanted to find out more about his relationship with Josh Richards and Thomas Mandell, the driver of the truck who was about to be tried in Dane County for manslaughter in the death of Tanner Mortenson. He was charged with reckless driving under the influence. He could get up to ten years since he qualified as an adult.

BEFORE I COULD question Kurt about the all night graduation party, Tara approached me as she was turning in her books to the English department the following Wednesday.

"I need to talk to you."

"Okay, how about tonight?"

"No, now. It's important."

"Well, okay, what's up?"

"Come with me to the classroom across the hall. Nobody's in there."

"So? What is it?"

"You know Kiki Bender."

"I don't really know her but I know she's one of the Kin."

"Yeah, well she was one of the girls at the Richards debauch Memorial weekend."

"Before you start. Was Kurt Buford there?" I asked, dreading the answer.

"He was, but he bounced. He and Dorene had a squabble and he left."

"Okay, thanks. What do you want to tell me."

"She went up there because Terry Alden invited her. She wishes she hadn't. Terry does too. They didn't stay when they saw what was going on."

"What was going on?"

"Do you know Marvin Coleman, the councilman?"

"Yes, I know who he is."

"He was with Dorene Hinton. She's sure of it. They went off together, maybe to a cabin. Everyone was drinking and sniffing something. She doesn't know what. And Lonnie Pepper started hitting on her and Terry got mad and punched him and they fought and Terry yelled at him to "get your fucking hands off her," meaning Kiki. He was so mad. He took her hand and they ran to the car. It was dark."

"I'm so sorry. Is she okay?"

"Yes," she said, but she was trembling when she said it.

"So why did Terry go up there?"

"Kurt invited him. Kurt and Terry and Kiki drove together and left together."

"Why are you telling me this?"

"Because you've been hanging out with Kurt and he was into Dorene until that day and now he's with you and I don't know what was going on but Kurt wasn't a part of it. Also Kiki is a witness to some dark. She may be in deep."

"All right, this is what I know. We saw Coleman with Dorene when we were in Cub Foods up there but we didn't know what that meant. So what it looked like was what it was. Maybe there's more to it."

"You think?"

"I think."

"Thanks for telling me." I put my arm around her shoulder as if I had known her for years. "Wendy and I have said that Kiki needs a friend. She has one in you and apparently in Terry."

I thought about how in the short time we had been in Buford Post, the glossy image of the town had proven to be a veneer to cover up rotting wood. I hoped it was not Buford wood, but it wasn't out of the question even though Kurt seemed to be absolved of the Memorial weekend debauchery. Coleman might not be convicted but surely he'd be dismissed from office. If I were his wife, I'd divorce him. He couldn't expect this affair to remain secret. Was Kiki in danger? Terry? I didn't trust Lonnie Pepper for a moment. I had to talk with Wendy.

I TEXTED HER and started walking. She picked me up and we drove to my home and looked for Dad who was standing in the vineyard admiring his grapes. We walked toward him, but I stopped and held Wendy back. "Look at him, Wendy. He's a man in his glory. Let's let him be for a while. He'll come in soon."

We watched as he moved among the rows of vines pausing to feel the leaves and touch the grapes beginning to bud. He moved with such calm and inner joy that was as easy to detect as a cardinal's whistle. We let him be.

When he came through the door, I asked him if he had time to talk. He did. "First, Dad, I'm so happy for you and for us. To see you in the vineyard nurturing the plants is a joy."

"Thank you, Sweetheart, that means a lot to me. I know you enjoy it, too."

"Yes, unfortunately Wendy and I want to discuss some new information with you."

We told him, everything we'd learned, especially about Coleman.

Dad was livid. "What the hell is he thinking having an affair with an 18 year old girl? He's married, has a daughter, and sits on the city council. Hinton suspected as much when I told him I saw them together. Anything can happen."

Dad had no more to say for the moment. He, too, realized what was at stake. Was this the whole story or was it only the opening chapters. And what about Millie, Coleman's 15 year old daughter, who hadn't been a part of any of this? How terrible for her to find out about her father's unseemly behavior. She'd be a junior next year. How would she cope?

Dad decided to talk with Westin and Odegaard about what we'd learned to decide on whatever action had to be taken. They were as shocked as we were, and angry at Coleman, while doubting Kurt, and worried about what Hinton might do. And what about Dorene? Was she a flighty school girl enamored by a town councilman or was she some kind of femme fatale using her wiles to bring down, an honorable man? And what was really going on up there in Riverton?

We decided to do nothing about Coleman at that point and not worry about Hinton. The next move was for Dad and me to drive to Riverton and talk with the DNR there. Surely, they had to know something about any illegal cutting and improper waste disposal and maybe even some illicit behavior that the police might like to know about. I wanted Wendy to join us, whom I hadn't seen in a few days, but she declined because she had acquired a summer job working at the reception desk at Swanson's Resort. I was surprised. She hadn't said anything about it in our brief texts. Strange.

It was now the middle of June and cloudy with threats of thunder storms and possible high winds with hail, but we went anyway. Rain slapped the windshield of the Prius making it difficult to converse. I played video games. I didn't remember what because my mind kept wandering. I peered through the rain streaking across the side windows to watch the pines and birches waving in the wind as if they were fans at a football game or greeters at a major forestry event. We'd see how welcome we were.

We found the Department of Natural Resources office on that Wednesday afternoon and were shown to the office of Roger Fairweather, DNR forester with whom we had made an appointment.

Cordially, he inquired the nature of our business, sensing the matter was of some significance. Dad began.

"Do you know of any investigations of improper lumbering going on at the Richards estate?"

"You understand, of course, that I can't give you specific information regarding any of our investigations, but I can say that there have been some."

"Involving the Richards?"

"Yes, but no incriminating information has been found. There was a young man from your area here last fall taking water samples of the Wisconsin River and feeding creeks to determine the degree of pollutants that may be coming from the paper mill. I assisted him in finding significant areas where such waste might best be detected. He intended to come back to do some more tests. But then we heard of his death. What a shame. Such a fine young man."

"Do you think he was on to something?"

"It could be. We haven't followed up throughout the winter, but we need to get on it again. He had credibility even though he hadn't finished his tests.

"Do you remember his name?" My dad asked.

I was on the edge of my chair by this time, sure of what he was about to say.

"Yes, I have it right here on the calendar from last September. Hayward Russell. He had been here a couple of times during the summer before he started testing."

"He was my biology teacher," I asserted. "He wanted major action to prevent climate change and protested the relaxed guidelines that allow improper discharge into our waterways."

"Tell us what you know about the Richards company," Dad said.

"As far as we know the company has always operated within the guidelines, but, as you know, the guidelines are quite liberal."

"Meaning?"

"Meaning cutting on private property is pretty much up to the property owner. Of course, stripped branches and chips need to be removed to prevent fire and pests."

"And as far as you know they have followed those guidelines?"

"As far as we know. I know that Buford Lumber buys a lot of wood from Richards and helps him distribute it to several other mills. But all businesses have suffered from the economic downturn. I don't know how well these two businesses have faired."

I had to speak. "Is it possible that Mr. Russell was probing into matters that might upset one or both of the businesses?"

"I haven't considered any foul play. But it is possible that the data he was collecting could cause these companies to face fines and changes in their processing that could cost them big money. After all the Wisconsin River is a major flow through the state way down into Iowa, and all the towns down river will scream if they believe that a factory is endangering our water."

"You said that you would 'get on it again.' Does that mean that you will carry out the testing or do you hire out a lab technician from somewhere? Dad asked."

"The latter. We hire technicians from the State Tech College."

"The point is these businesses could suffer from too much probing," I said.

"Well, yes, if their findings are significant."

With that we thanked Mr. Fairweather for his information and concern, and Dad asked that he keep us informed of any findings.

"Sure. I'll do that but we probably won't be doing any tests for a few weeks and then it'll take another week or two to analyze the results."

"We understand," Dad said, but I didn't. Why didn't Fairweather see this as high priority? If that mill was polluting, shouldn't we know about it asap? I was frustrated. I was also disturbed to find out a motive for Russell's beating, that the thugs who did it were put up to it to give him a warning. We had something more than Coleman to consider—unless he was involved someway beyond having an affair with Dorene. Dad said that when he talked to Hinton and mentioned that his daughter was with Coleman up north Coleman called him a "Son of a Bitch." Immediately he assumed the worst. Why? I know it looked suspicious, but wouldn't he give a councilman and leader of the community the benefit of the doubt. But no, it appeared he jumped to the same conclusion we did. Maybe Coleman had a dark history known to at least a few in the community.

Now we were off to the Anderson's place for the evening and further considerations. The rain had stopped. The wind had died. The clouds floated east leaving the sky open to the west where the sun eased its way down behind the pines. It was beautiful, with temperature in the low 70's.

I hated Coca Cola. I really did, but I didn't say so, because that's what we were offered the last time we were here and what I had with Kurt at the Watering Hole. I suggested we make lemonade, but Maia and I had to make it ourselves. The adults drank Chardonnay.

"I don't see why WE can't take samples of the river and take them to the lab. That would speed things up," I remarked thoughtfully.

"Hold on, hold on," Anderson puts in, if what you suspect is true, I suggest you engage the authorities."

"We did, the DNR, aren't they the authorities?" I asked.

Dad suggested that Anderson take us to where the river runs by the paper mill, and places down stream a few miles. There we could take samples in glass jars that Anderson still had from days of canning their home grown tomatoes and apple sauce from their Harrelson apple trees. But before we did Dad wanted to search the Web for information on both Buford Lumber and the

Richards business interests. He mapped out the entire Richards 7,000 acre forest and the backroad that could take us to different parts and to the state and federal land surrounding it.

So the three of us did our sneaky investigation and collection of water samples. Sneaky because we had to get inside the paper mill property without detection since the NO TRESPASSING signs made it quite clear that no one enters without permission. And why shouldn't we get permission?

"Because," Anderson said, "they may not allow sampling without a warrant or they may direct us to areas they want us to sample, which, of course, defeats our purpose."

"And what if we're caught?" I wondered.

"They can have us arrested for trespassing."

"Oh," I swallowed hard. Dad thought we could talk our way out of it with some yet-to-be-considered explanation.

"Well, okay, let's do it," I felt the adrenaline now.

None of the three of us had figured out how to get past the signs. Of course an attendant sat in the gate guardhouse to check all entries. But we had no intention to go through the gate. We parked a few blocks from that entrance just over the Wisconsin River bridge as if we planned to fish as a couple of teenagers were doing. I hoped those fish weren't too polluted to eat. Just beyond, the chain link fence topped off with barbed wire, a sure deterrent to a fence climber. I could see that entry was not to be. That was water under the bridge, I thought. Exactly, we would sample the water under the bridge. Any pollutants found would have to be from the paper mill less than a mile up the road. Both Dad and Anderson collected a full jar and screw on the tops. Now to deliver it, but not to the Northern Tech Lab. Rather to the environmental studies college of Eau Claire University.

We did that on our way home. The lab technicians promised they would send the results to us and to Mr. Fairweather of the DNR in Riverton. It would take a couple of weeks. So we waited.

I TEXTED WENDY to report on our detective adventures, but she didn't respond. I left her a message to call me. But she didn't call. That Wednesday evening I called her again and she said she couldn't talk while at work. "I'm sorry, Libby," she said, "I have to hang up 'cause there's a customer waiting. I'll call you tomorrow." But she didn't call. That was unlike her. We were best friends. So I waited, a bit lonely.

On the other hand, I had my summer laid out for me to assist with the grape farm, as I called it. Dad called it a vineyard. I guess that's what it was. I checked the ground around the plants for water and made sure that frameworks supported each vine. Also I measured the hours of sunshine each day as the summer progressed as well as sun vs. cloud cover and rainfall. I kept a log of all this data for future reference, so that we could compare year to year to match with the grape yield. I liked my job and Dad paid me twelve dollars an hour for my labors most of which I saved for a car. By the time the lab report came in, I would have my driver's license and would need money for gas that cost at a little over two dollars a gallon.

In the meantime and in the evenings I quite often saw Kurt who had made it quite clear that I was his girl. No more Dorene. I wanted to believe him. It seemed that he was keeping his word. I asked about her every once in a while, but he said he knew nothing of her activities. I wondered if he knew about Coleman. I wouldn't tell him what I thought I knew. I wanted so much for Kurt to be real. I liked the way he smelled and the way he touched my face as if petting a bird. When he held me gently, I longed for his kiss. I was almost begging. Would I survive without him in the fall? I'd never felt like this, this longing. It frightened me. The end of June approached. August first he'd be joining the preseason football team at the U.

WENDY CALLED ME Friday morning. About time. She said she had to talk with me immediately, now. "I'm coming over," she said.

I told Dad I'd be late getting started at the vineyard and he made it clear I had no schedule. Wendy, trying to hold back tears, plopped down on the sofa and took the glass of water I offered her. Her nose puffed red and her eyes teared.

"It was terrible," she said. "Last night about 10 o'clock three guys walked in. I greeted them with a smile thinking they wanted to reserve a room. I thought I recognized one. I tried to think from where. Of course it was from the party on that houseboat party last fall. One guy said, 'Isn't it dangerous for a pretty noob like you to be working here all alone at night. You have such a pretty little nose. It's too bad it gets fucking stuck in places it doesn't belong. It might end up in deep shit.'"

She sobbed now and I held her close.

"I knew I was in trouble so I pushed the alarm button under the counter that sounded in the Swanson home. Then two of them came around the counter, and one grabbed my arm while the other took hold of my nose and twisted hard until it bled. I screamed. It hurt so bad and I thought they would kill me. Then they scooted out the door. Swanson and his wife ran in, alarmed, and she yelled, 'What happened? Have we been robbed?'"

"I couldn't talk, still sobbing, blood dripping all over my blouse, but I managed to say, 'I don't think so.'"

"And he said, 'You're bleeding.'"

"If I weren't so scared, I would have laughed, Well, duh.

"Swanson said, 'I don't think it's broken. It was foolish of me to think you should take the night shift. It never dawned on me you could be in danger.' Mrs. came back with some ice and held it to my nose.

"Ohhh. It hurt. But the greater hurt was that someone would do that to me."

"My, God, Wendy, I'm so sorry. Are you going to be all right?" I consoled.

"I think so, but I'm really shook."

"So you think one of the guys you recognized. Would you be able to identify him?"

"I'm sure. He was the one twisting my nose."

"They said you are sticking your nose where it doesn't belong?"

"Yes. They're warning us, Libby. Be careful. You may be next."

"What do we do now?"

"I told my parents and Dad is looking into it. He conferred with the Swansons who agree that I should have a few days off then work during the day with constant supervision. They're nice people who never thought anything like this would happen. They don't understand it. They weren't robbed. I don't tell them what the guy said so they don't know about our investigations. Dad, of course, is more sure than ever that our probing is pricking the skin of raw flesh. He didn't say it that way, but that's what he meant. 'No more detective for you,'" he said. "I'm really tired. I have to go."

I held her as we walked to the door when Dad walked in and saw Wendy's face. "What happened Wendy? He stuttered. He held her at arms length.

"She has to go, Dad, I'll tell you about it."

After I helped her to the door, i told him all. I shook as I imagined those hoodlums could attack me. It might even be worse for me. "I'm scared, Dad."

"Yes, it's okay." He held me. Then I went to my room and lay down. I calmed myself with deep breaths and woke up around noon. I had no intention of quitting the investigtation, but I had to be cautious, not take chances.

I thought about Kiki Bender. I'd never talked with her beyond a greeting, but I thought I needed to for her sake and for mine. Tara gave me her phone number. When she learned it was me calling I sensed her caution. "Yes, Hi, why are you calling?" She almost whispered as if surrounded by eavesdroppers.

"Kiki, I know we don't know each other, but Tara has told me about the Richards Estate ordeal and I want you to know that I support you and feel sorry you had to experience such unseemly behavior. I'd like to get together with you to talk. As you know I've been seeing Kurt, but I'm not sure he's legit. I'd like to know everything you have observed with the Kin and especially that Memorial weekend. Will you talk to me about what you know?"

"Maybe, I'm a little bummed out 'cause I don't know what's going on."

"Will you meet with me?"

"I guess so. Where?"

"How about at Lucy's?"

We met there on Friday afternoon after I assured Dad that I was caught up on my work. We both ordered lemonades.

After I told her what Tara related, she withdrew deeply into the booth as if cowering from some fairytale ogre.

"What are you thinking?" I probed.

"I'm thinking that you need to quit investigating. You're pressing important people. You could get hurt."

"You mean like Wendy last night?"

"What happened to Wendy?"

I told her. "What happened between Kurt and Dorene on Memorial Weekend?"

"I don't know if I should tell you."

"Please I need to know."

"I suppose you do." She paused to gather her thoughts and to find the right words to begin. "Kurt isn't the all-American boy that everyone thinks he is."

"Tell me."

"You know I've been Dorene's friend for over a year. She pulls us girls in like a magnet. We are an exclusive club that lives on the edge we teeter on. She has had the hots for Kurt for as long as I have known her. Kurt hangs out with her, you know, but not just her. He took up with Rosy Masters and even hit on my friend Tara until she left the crew. She didn't want to play Dorene's games."

"What are Dorene's games?"

Again she withdrew for a moment and returned looking me in the eyes. "Sex," she said. "They're all players. Pick a guy and fuck him. She picked Kurt and I picked Lonnie Pepper. Kurt came on to me, too, but I knew he was Dorene's property so I stayed away from him."

"So why did Kurt come on to me?" I asked confused.

"To make Dorene jealous. They see themselves as the King and Queen, and the rest of us as their subjects and he wants you as part of his court. At first Dorene saw you as a threat. Then she wanted you in so she could control you, but then you were gaining too much popularity with that global warming shit."

"So who wrote SLUT on my locker?"

"I did."

"Why?

"Dorene told me to. I'm sorry. She doesn't sucker me anymore."

"So why did she and Kurt break up?"

"Because he saw that she had gone for bigger fish. She brought Kurt down."

"What do you mean bigger fish?"

"I think you know."

"Who? Coleman?"

She didn't respond, just looked at me with that "You said it," kind of look.

"Why him?"

"Something to do with the Richards, I think."

"So what's Kurt's interest in the Richards?"

"I don't know exactly, but you know Buford Lumber gets most of its wood supplies from them and Kurt and his father, go up to Riverton from time to time to do business, I guess. That's how he knows Josh, who is a real douchebag and constantly high."

In the few minutes since we had began our conversation she had become a motor mouth as if she had wanted to get bottled up stuff from exploding from her chest.

Suddenly she stopped. "If you tell anybody what I'm telling you, please don't say where you got the information. I could be in real trouble."

"Like Hayward Russell?"

She knocked over the lemonade that she had hardly touched.

"What are you talking about?"

"You know, don't you."

She stammered, shook her head that seemed like a No then a nod like a Yes, but more like a swarm of gnats had attacked her.

"Fuck, I'm spewing shit."

Lucy came with a towel to wipe up the spill and smiled. "You two are having quite a conversation, it seems. Is everything all right."

We both smiled. Kiki said, "Fine."

I tried to bring the conversation back to what she was willing to say.

"You and Lonnie became an item."

"For a while, but I didn't like the way he treated me. One time—at that Valentines bash at the Hintons we — you were there —and then we left for a party in Sterling. It got pretty steamy and Lonnie got rough with me. I don't like that kind of sex, so I smacked him hard and he smacked me. That was the end of it. Kurt and Dorene took me home. I haven't been out with him since."

"Now you're with Terry Alden?"

Her face brightened. She broke into a smile, a lovely smile like a girl reborn. "Yes," she said, "He's never been a part of any of these parties. He sat next to me in algebra and we started talking and he's so sweet and nice and he asked me out, so we've been going together since early March. We haven't had sex but we were going to at the Memorial party at the Richards. Then Lonnie hit on me. You know. Tara told you, right?"

"Yes, she did. But why did you take Terry up there?"

"He took me, because Kurt invited him and he knew I was a friend of Dorene. Dorene is still my friend, sort of, I mean she's been trying to get me back in with Lonnie but I've kept my distance, so she's been kinda cool to me, but I don't want to lose her as a friend. Well, maybe I do. I don't know."

I made another stab at it. "You do know who beat up Hayward Russell, don't you."

"Look, you've got to lay off. It's real complicated and dangerous."

"I think there's another reason you broke up with Lonnie Pepper."

Again Kiki was speechless.

"I think you found out that Lonnie was one of the guys who jumped him."

Nothing. Then she blurted, "We're done talking."

She was visibly upset, fidgeting as if she had to leave then settling back as though she wanted to stay, scratching at her leg. I thought she may scream or cry or laugh hysterically. Instead she grew rigid and stared at me as if I had assaulted her. Maybe I had. I'd broken into her vulnerability and she tried to collect the pieces of herself. What she knew had become a huge burden for her.

"I really like Terry," she pulled her comment from the ceiling. It appeared she wanted a good relationship and was fighting herself to break from adventures gone wrong. I imagined her struggle but couldn't comprehend it. I could see she didn't want to be who she had become. She didn't want Terry to know about her. Yet she went with him to Riverton daring herself to tell him. Lonnie's behavior and Terry's defense of her caused that revelation not to happen. They left and obviously she didn't tell him about her past with Lonnie. At that moment I felt like a real detective, putting two and two together. I hoped they didn't add up to five.

"Please, don't tell anyone what we've been talking about."

I didn't promise. I couldn't, but I would be careful whom I'd tell. No one needed to know that she wrote on my locker or that Lonnie was one of the Russell's assailants. We already knew that. I didn't need to tell anyone about Kurt. What our investigation needed was information about the Buford/Richards deals. We could probe into that. I doubted that Wendy would be detective anymore. She was scared. Frankly, so was I and Tara and Kiki and probably several others. Something more was going on. That was for us to find out.

I HAD TO pry information out of Kurt. No more pretending that I was the only one he loved. No more drowning in his sweet talk. No more wanting his kisses. That would be hard. His kisses and arms felt good. But no more. He must not know that I had talked with Kiki. I had to get the information I wanted from him so that what I knew came from him.

I declined another boat trip on the river. Instead we met at Lucy's. My resistance upset him, especially my change in demeanor. I told him I had a lot to do on the grape farm and hadn't the time or energy for a night on the river. I smiled so he'd think he knew what I meant by "energy." That seemed to relax him. On a Saturday night Lucy's was packed with people enjoying happy hour at only 5:30. We couldn't hold a conversation without yelling. Since I didn't want my questions and his answers heard, I suggested we leave. We couldn't talk straight down there.

The restaurant at Swanson's resort offered the quiet necessary for intimate conversation with only a few patrons. When we arrived, Billy Olson, emerged from the office, said Hi and headed for his car. I stopped him. "What are you doing here, Billy?" I asked puzzled.

"I work here. It's my summer job to be grounds keeper and help with cleaning the rooms."

"Wendy works here, too," I said.

"Yes, she was receptionist on the nightshift until she had a terrible scare, so now she works days and I check up on her often. She's great. We've had some good talks and done some silly stuff together." He chuckled.

I could tell that the two of them had hit it off together. Jealousy rose in me like a heat wave. I'd always thought that Billy was my escape door from Kurt, if I needed to use it. Maybe not. Maybe she had been so distant for a while because she was dating Billy and didn't want me to know. Why? Maybe because she thought she had taken Billy's interest away from me, even though I'd been focused on Kurt. I needed to let her know I was happy for her.

We found a booth and Kurt began, "What was Wendy's terrible scare?"

At first my thoughts about Wendy distracted me. I refocused. I told him what happened to her and he seemed concerned. "Is she okay?"

"Her nose will recover, but her spirit will heal more slowly. Tell me something. What do you have to do with the Richards?"

"What do you mean? Our company buys most of our wood supplies from them and what they don't have they get for us from other wood cutters. My dad and I go up there from time to time to place orders."

"You know Josh Richards quite well, I take it."

"Enough to socialize a little bit. You're thinking about him and his friend at the basketball tournament, aren't you. That didn't turn out so well."

"No, it didn't. You lost one of your best friends to a stupid driving exhibition. But you still went back up to Riverton for the Memorial Day party."

"I already told you about that. It was a mistake and I tanked it with Dorene."

"But you have had sex with her many times. Right?"

"What's this all about, anyway? That's all over and done with. I'm with you now."

"So why did you break up with her? Tell me the truth."

"She was banging some other guy."

"That isn't so unusual for her, is it?"

"Shit, Libby, leave it alone."

"Who was the guy, Kurt?"

"I don't know, some guy."

"Like maybe Marvin Coleman."

"What? You mean the councilman?"

"Doesn't he work for Buford Lumber?"

"Yeah, he's a marketer."

"And he's fucking Dorene Hinton. And you know more about her, too, don't you. Last fall Hayward Russell was not in a bar fight in spite of what the rumor is. You know that, don't you. He was beaten on his door step and you know it."

"No I don't. I don't know what you're talking about.'"

"Yes, you do. Did you have something to do with that? I have evidence to prove one of the guys involved and you know who they are."

"Where are you getting this shit?"

"I have my sources."

"Listen, Libby, leave it alone."

"And if I don't?"

"Just leave it alone."

"I can't spend time with you if you won't be straight with me. Maybe you are protecting criminals. Maybe you're one of them. Why do you think they beat on Russell? Tell me what you know."

"No." he stammered.

"No, you won't tell me or no you don't know why?"

"No, I don't know why."

"You're not telling me the truth, Kurt. Take me home."

The waiter stood before us asking if we intended to order.

"No," I said. "We're leaving."

At his Fusion he grabbed me, whirled me around and tried to force a kiss. I brought my right leg up as hard as I could into his groin. He clutched himself and rolled on the ground.

"God damn you," he moaned.

I ran back into Swanson's and told the waiter to call the cops. Kurt didn't come in. I saw through the window that he had driven off. The waiter called the police and told them everything was all right, but they came anyway so I had to tell them what happened. They said I had to tell them his name. I tried to avoid it, but they insisted. When they heard, Kurt Buford, they looked startled. The shortest one said, "We'll look into it." But I knew they wouldn't. Neither of the officers wanted to put Kurt on record, not the town, high school hero. I didn't know if I was relieved or anxious. If it were anybody else, they would have found him and questioned him at the least.

I called my dad and asked him to come and get me, that I'd explain when he arrived. God, how stupid could I be to hand out all my evidence on a silver platter. If he had been using me and intending to seduce me, he now knew that I had been using him to get information that might incriminate him, his friends, his dad's company, the Richards, Dorene. He never answered my question about Dorene, but I was sure she figured into all this somewhere.

When Dad arrived, I told him all. "My God, what were you thinking?" Dad exclaimed.

"I don't know Dad. I guess I was impatient. I wanted answers and I believed he had some."

"That's enough detective work. As Kurt said, 'Leave it alone.' Any more investigating needs to be done by the authorities, not us. I have your safety to think about."

"I know. I'm scared."

In the middle of the week we received the results of our water samples. They reported toxicity to the danger point, far above acceptable. Then the DNR called. Mr. Fairweather said they intended to continue the investigation with a warrant to determine the source of the pollution and issue warnings and timeline for clean up. Fines would be imposed. Plus they intended to analyze the vapor pouring from the paper mill smoke stack for atmospheric pollution. And they assigned their undercover agent to continue probing into the Richards harvesting procedures and waste disposal. He had already collected some data that was concerning and he would continue to do so. He thanked us for our sampling and concern and asked us to let the DNR handle the case from here on.

It was clear that someone threatened by Hayward Russell's investigation persuaded a couple of guys to warn him with their fists. Why Lonnie Pepper and whoever else? What was their interest in the Richards business? There had to be something more to it. Let the DNR go about their investigation. We still had unsolved mysteries here and my summertime boyfriend was somehow involved. I doubt, however, that after my accurate kick he would have anything to do with me unless in revenge. I didn't know what he was capable of and I didn't want to find out.

On Thursday he called. I knew better than to discuss any of the information we had received and just listened. He apologized for forcing himself on me and tried to explain that he was so angry with me for ruining our time together by spewing so much false information. He said that Dorene was the only one he had sex with in spite of what some might think and it was true that he flirted with me to make Dorene jealous. It was also true that Dorene and her friends were promiscuous but he was trying to change that. Then he said I was completely wrong about who the guy was that she was into now. That guy really pissed me off. He was never a real friend but I got to know him because of our lumber company dealings. "Are you listening?"

"Yes, I'm listening. So who is it then that she's fucking now?"

"Holy Christ, I've never heard you talk like this before. What's happening to you?"

"I think the question is what's happening to you. Why would you stay with a girl who's the real slut? And why are you protecting her? What has she got on you?"

"I just want to forget about her. It's you I want."

"Why me? There are others that may be more to your liking, like Rosy Masters or Kiki Bender. (I mentioned Kiki to make him think Kiki was still one of them, to derail his train of thought.) And how can you be friends with Lonnie Pepper? As much as I've enjoyed our time together, I don't trust you. I don't know what to believe about you. I don't know who you are. The great athlete, yes, no one disputes that and because you've brought honor to the town, no one wants to believe that you have a dark side, that you may be involved in some bad stuff. Before I can spend anymore time with you, you have to tell me all."

"I've told you all I can. You have to trust me."

"God dammit, Kurt. Don't you get it? You want me to care for you but you won't level with me. How can I? Sorry." I hung up.

IN A MONTH Kurt left for Madison. We hadn't talked. It was over between us. I hadn't learned anything more. I prepared for my junior year, practicing my clarinet for auditions, out of the detective business as Dad demanded. I was tired of it anyway. Wendy and I played duets together and established a woodwind quintet with flute, French horn, bassoon and Wendy on oboe and me on clarinet. Our band director, Mr. Sullivan, lent us music from the school archives to practice. I had no boyfriend, which had never bothered me before, but it did now, a bit, because Wendy had Billy Olson. Sorry, but I wished it were me. I tried not to be jealous. Their relationship wouldn't hurt our friendship, because I had no claims on him. I just knew that he had been interested in me ever since our lab class together while I was fantasizing about Kurt. Stupid me. God I hated hormones. I cleaned up my language. I didn't give a shit about Dorene. Sorry, didn't give a damn. Was that better, I wondered. She was leaving for Stout in Menominee soon to study whatever. No doubt, she would work for her dad on the docks some day until she marries some handsome deadbeat. Kiki Bender told me Dorene and Lonnie Pepper were hanging out together now and the two of them were going up to Riverton almost every weekend. Kiki was thick with Terry Alden, she said. She'd be a senior and head cheerleader, a real commitment. She was good. We, Wendy and I, began seeing her quite often. I liked her. She was a much nicer person now. She had a future. I didn't think Dorene did. But what did I know? Certainly not with Kurt who had probably found someone else, some college girl. So the graduates left and the Kin faded to nothing.

Sometimes in the night I woke and thought about the unsolved crimes. I still wanted to know who beat up our favorite teacher, what laws the Richards had broken, why the Sterling guys attacked Wendy, and what mischief Kurt was in. I knew one thing for sure: Lonnie Pepper was one of Russell's assailants. As far as I knew, Hinton had not "made it right" with Coleman. Maybe he had. If so, it hadn't reached the local paper. That's all

I had to go on and, of course, the indictments that might come from the Riverton DNR. On those nights I lay awake for hours before I rose and prepared for a full day in the vineyard. I called it the vineyard now. We had grapes, not a lot but the vines were doing well. I kept the statistics and showed my dad once a week so that he knew I was steadfast. Twice we'd had the Westins and Odegaards over for a three piece woodwind quintet concert. They loved it and we loved playing for them.

Sometimes I took out my clarinet and let my fingers discover what I played, one tune emerged and faded into another. I floated with the melodies as if carried on a breeze or a cloud. At times the tune turned dark in a minor key and took me down with it until the notes wept through me. They carried my sadness from what I'd learned. Buford Post looked so different to me now. So much I loved about it here and much made me cry. Kurt had drawn me into its darkness. I'd almost become accustomed to it, the darkness I mean. I expected it even on the brightest day. Like my shadow the darkness lay in wait before me.

I turned the notes around to a major key and the darkness lifted. Suddenly I played the school rouser as if in the marching band on the football field. My fingers froze on the final notes. I put my instrument away. My musical tour lifted my spirits as if it were a meditation. Perhaps it was. I talked to myself when I play like that. The music became the answer to my unspoken questions. Strange, but I hardly ever play the clarinet any more. I don't think I've picked it up in at least four years.

I loved the vineyard. Have I told you that? Walking among the vines I felt a part of the flowering of America. That might be silly, but that's how I felt. Just think, the fermented grape has been the drink of humanity for centuries and we are continuing the nectar of the gods. Hmmm. The nectar of the gods. I know some people drink too much of the stuff, but those who have developed a palate for the delicacies and the nose for the aroma of superb wine know that the intoxication comes from the ecstasy of life on this abundant planet. Of course I didn't know all of this in the early years of our vineyard when this story was in its infancy, but I do now. Now I know that the grape turned to wine is a blessing of life. My family knows it. I've learned that wine drinkers of quality wine, drink for its esthetic appeal, it's sense of connection to each other and the earth, and I love that. When I spend time at home in the summer I often offer samples of our wine to tourists in our tasting room. I couldn't be more proud to tease their palates.

Back then as I began my junior year, I was glad Kurt was gone. Gone, I say, Gone. Out of my life. I wished him no harm, but I believed he was my adversary. While the Buford Lumber Company had been an asset to the town for generations, it might no longer be an asset to the planet, to our human survival. To those who thought that climate change was a hoax, I said, "Your ignorance or your greed, whatever it is, that allows you to dismiss scientific reality, your neglect and continued support of false information is a danger to all of us." I was happy to continue my work in the science club, even though the interest had waned since Hayward Russell passed away. We wouldn't forget what he taught us. The situation grows worse as I write this. I wasn't sure that the lumber company was guiltless in adding to the problem.

I told you that I liked Kiki. Since she broke from the Kin and took up with Terry, she had become more friendly. She even hung out with Wendy and me, two lowly juniors, once in a while. Dad learned from the county sheriff in Camden that even if we had evidence that Lonnie Pepper was one of the assailants who beat up Russell, we didn't have a case because Russell was dead—not unless we brought a lawsuit against him. The police had no reason to pursue it, because there was no evidence that the beating caused his death. Chances were if brought in for questioning, Pepper would refuse to reveal his accomplices and certainly deny any charges brought against him. So that was that for the time being.

Kiki called me on a Saturday morning and said she wanted to talk. She came over and we sat in the porch overlooking out at the vineyard. It was a beautiful early autumn morning in bright sunlight and warm breeze. The grapes were full but not ripe. I loved to watch them swell with juice from day to day and still do. I said that to Kiki and she laughed at me for being silly, then turned sullen and looked me straight on.

She began, "The more we spend time together, I understand you and why you have pursued your investigation. It isn't only because of Russell's death. It's because you believe that he found evidence against the lumber company dealings with the Richards Forestry Company. Am I right?"

"Yes." I said no more, waiting for her make her point.

"Well." She paused what seemed like a century. I waited.

"You told me you have the photo that identifies Lonnie Pepper. We hung out together, and you know that. One time when we were partying with Corey Morissey and Dorene and Lonnie, and I don't know who else —I know Kurt wasn't there—Lonnie says to Corey, "We sure gave that fucking teacher something to think about, that Son of a bitch. Good fucking riddance."

"'And you were so cool, Dorene,'" Corey said.

"'Shit, all I did was drive the car.'"

"They laughed. 'And no one has a fucking clue.' Lonnie chuckled."

"I didn't say anything, but it made me sick. Really, Libby, I should have told somebody, you, maybe, a long time ago, but I was really bummed. Still I hung out with Lonnie until he started roughing me up. He was dragging me down. He made me feel like shit. Then I realized that I didn't have to put up with abuse, and broke it off. He pursued me, but, as scared as I was that he might hurt me, I stayed away from him. He was like a wolf after a deer. Terry helped me. He didn't know he helped me. He helped me by being Terry, a really nice guy who I could talk to. So now you know." She started to cry. "I'm so sorry."

"Holy shit," I blurted. "I wonder if Tara knows."

"I doubt it," she mumbled, "I'm sure he doesn't tell her anything. He wouldn't trust her to keep her mouth shut."

"I don't know what we can do about it now, except to figure out who put them up to it and why," I said, realizing Kiki had reopened the investigation, not into Russell's beating and death, but into what the instigators were afraid of. Kiki had joined our ranks to do what I didn't know, not yet anyway.

I haven't told you, but I will now, and you'll see why in a few words. Lucy had expanded her bar and grill to the property next door owned by REMAX Realty. The owners, whose names I didn't know, agreed to split their street front property to include a Starbucks Coffee Shop with connecting doors from the bar and grill through the coffee shop to the realty. All three ran from the street to the back porches overlooking the Hinton marina that stretched for three blocks along the riverfront then up the incline to the Amoco station and bait shop. Now customers could buy a meal at Lucy's and a drink or a cup of Starbuck's coffee and sit on the back porches in the summer in either place or they could engage a real estate agent over a repast. After the coffee shop and realty office closed at five p.m., a customer could call the number posted on window for a real estate appointment and have a cup of always brewing coffee or a drink from the bar while examining the offerings. Lucy did everything well.

So the reason I'm telling you this is that on opening day the second weekend in August, Kiki, Wendy and I went for free coffees of our choice while adults bought beers for fifty cents and the realty firm handed out Lucy's specially made sticky buns. We discovered that Tara Morissey had been hired for the rest of the summer and then after school to make and sell coffee, also to open at six a.m. on Saturday and Sunday mornings. Good for her. I decided to drop in some late afternoon when the coffee shop served only the few customers who sat along the wall with their computers. I wanted to ask her about her brother.

Tuesday afternoon about three o'clock I ordered an iced coffee to which I added lots of cream. I wasn't really a coffee drinker yet, but I made exceptions to be sociable. I asked her if she had a moment to talk and she did but might have to jump up to serve a customer.

"Sure, no problem," I said.

"So what's up?" She asked.

"I'm wondering about your brother. The last I heard he was planning on going to Eau Claire University. Is that right?"

"Why do you ask?"

"It's just that I haven't seen him around since early summer and wonder how he's doing."

"No, he's not going to college this fall. He decided to take a year off from school and continues working up north for the Richards. He works on a cutting crew, I understand." She looked distressed as she spoke "To tell you the truth we haven't heard from him in quite a while. I've texted him but he hasn't responded. I'm worried about him."

I didn't say, 'you should be,' but that was what I thought. Kiki had never told her about her brother's illicit involvement in the Russell incident.

"We've never agreed on much but I've always felt close to him. I miss him."

'Oh my God. What she didn't know might turn out to be worse than she thought. We talked about school and how she hoped to go into real estate after she graduated next year. I knew she was a good student, but she wasn't interested in college. We parted with hugs and wished each other well with a "See you in school."

That was what I figured. I told Kiki about our conversation and she nodded knowingly. "I think we know what to investigate. I don't think Wendy will join us."

"No," I said, "her interests have turned to Billy Olson."

We made plans, secretive plans, Kiki and I, nobody else for the weekend before school started. I told Dad and Mom that Kiki and I wanted to go camping at Trempealeau State Park if it was all right with them. It was, but that wasn't where we went. I think it was the first time I had deceived them. I didn't feel right about it, but I knew if they knew our plan they wouldn't allow it. I didn't intend to include Wendy, but I knew she would excuse herself anyway because she was going to Wisconsin Dells for the weekend with the Olson family. I wished it were me. No I didn't. Actually during summer band I'd hit if off a bit with Larry Rappaport, trumpet player, and straight A liberal. What wasn't to like?

Sometimes I hated myself. I seemed to live a charmed life while others around me suffered from family woes, or broken relationships, or dangerous temptations. Okay, I admit that my infatuation for Kurt was a downer, but it wasn't like he was the only one for me. As Mom said there were more fish in the sea, but why did I want a fish? And why did he keep popping up in my thoughts when I wanted nothing to do with him? Maybe I needed a psychiatrist. No, not really. I needed to forget him. But what if he was innocent and I had accused him of promiscuity and criminal behavior. Who did I think I was? Sometimes I hated myself. Sometimes I thought I was some kind of guru and expected all my friends to sit at my feet in worship. Maybe I was more like Dorene that I knew, except for the sex. Why did she do that? Did she do it to feel needed? How could that help her self-esteem? If I could have trusted Kurt's affection, I might have had sex with him. I was that close. I was a detective and I played the clarinet. Bully for me. Maybe I was just a pretty object like a statue in the city park. We didn't have one, a statue, I mean. We had the park. Maybe I should go stand there for people to gaze at and say in passing or as they walked around me for a three dimensional view, "Isn't she pretty?" Yes, I was. I was pretty. What else was I?

Kiki drove her yellow Hyundai that showed a few dents but ran well. The day started out with beautiful sunshine at eight in the morning and a mild temperature of 75 degrees, but it clouded up three quarters of the way to Riverton and stayed that way with only a mild threat of rain. A few of the aspen trees showed signs of autumn color and in a week or two almost overnight would burst with color.

I love fall. The air takes on a crispness that stimulates me to perform. Back then I seemed to play my clarinet better, sleep better, even smile more. Not that I don't enjoy the warm summers, but the aura of autumn captivates me in a special way. That fall day I was bursting with energy because of the task ahead of us.

Kiki, on the other hand, seemed sullen, removed maybe, as if she was somewhere else. I let her be for awhile. I noticed she scratched her arms a lot, sometimes her legs. I recalled she did that the last time we talked at Lucy's open house. I didn't mention it, but after a period of her morose silence, I asked, "Is everything ok?"

"Sure, why do you ask?"

"You seem far away,"

"Oh, I'm thinking about starting my senior year next week. I don't know if I'm ready."

"I'm sure it'll go fine."

She offered a weak smile, then retreated into herself.

"I have to make a rest stop," she said as she pulled into a Phillip's station. She disappeared into the restroom and I called Dad. When he answered I apologized for not telling him the truth and explained where we were and what we were up to. The truth was that I didn't know exactly what we were up to. In fact, I wasn't feeling good about it all of a sudden. Kiki didn't seem herself. She seemed agitated. Maybe she was nervous about our investigation, but she was the one who seems so confident in what to look for and where exactly to go. I told Dad about my misgivings.

Af first he was angry then concerned. He explained that he received another report from the DNR and that they had found unusual toxins in the river water. They were amping up their investigations and warned us about further interference. He told me to turn around and come home. I didn't see how I could and that I'd call him soon. I was nervous now. I didn't know what we were doing.

Kiki returned full of energy like her old self it seemed. She exclaimed about what a lovely day it was in spite of the clouds.

"Aren't you the exuberant one. By the way, have you told Terry about our suspicions and our plans today?"

"No, no, he wouldn't approve. Besides I haven't seen him for a while."

"Really? I thought you two had something good going."

"Well, we curved. That's over." She passed it off as if it were water over the dam and of no consequence. Quite a turn around considering her earlier euphoria over Terry. I started probing. I worried that I was one stupid detective with no plan for an escape.

"So what do you think we'll find at the Richards place?

"I think you'll be surprised."

I was beginning to think so, too. I told her I needed a rest stop. She looked at me suspiciously and reminded me we had just made a stop. Now I was anxious. But she pulled over at a filling station in some little town feigning good humor, as she eyed me curiously.

"I'll be right back," I said. I left a message for Dad. "If you don't hear from me in twenty minutes call Anderson and the police. Send them to the Richards place.

Kiki didn't drive to the front gate but circled around to the east. I could see the lake. We were obviously entering on the north side.

"Where are we going?" I asked as calmly as I could.

"You'll see."

"So you've been here before."

"Oh, yeah."

"What's happening? I don't recall this as part of the plan."

"What do think our fucking plan is?"

"I really don't know. I put my trust in you."

"Stoop."

My heart had taken off at break neck speed. I hoped Dad got my message. We found a rough logging lane and turned south toward what must be the lake. The main entrance to the Richards estate was on the south side. I knew that.

We came to a lone cabin camouflaged by trees on the lake side. No one in a boat would know it was there. I smelled something like gasoline.

"What's that smell?" I probe.

"I don't smell anything."

"You can't smell that?" I saw trash bins full of plastic bottles and cans. As we approached the cabin, we were greeted by Lonnie Pepper, Corey Morissey and Dorene Hinton. I knew I was in trouble. I could only find out how much by remaining calm. I was sure now that Kiki wasn't on my side.

Lonnie gave Kiki a big hug. Dorene had her arm around Corey and gave me the you're-in-my-power look.

"Well, well, well, look who's here by special delivery. Quite the detective aren't you, my pretty." I didn't feel like Snow White. "I'm sure you've had a great trip with Kiki. You'll have even a better one soon. You're gonna love it," Dorene spouted She was giddy like a kid on her birthday surrounded by balloons. When I took out my cell phone, Lonnie grabbed it.

"There's no fucking service up here. You won't need this." He said with a wry chuckle. "We're going to have a fucking party in your honor."

"What's going on?" I tried to keep from screaming.

"You have any idea how much money you are going to cost this lumber company with your probing?"

I knew there was no point in answering his questions.

"It could be millions, but you're going down with us," said Josh Richards as he leaped from the cabin steps. He ran to me and grabbed both of my shoulders as I attempted to escape his grasp. "By the time you get out of here, you'll want me for your best friend." He laughed like the Joker in Batman. "Come inside. We have a little gift for you. We'll get you up to speed, crank you up so you can see over the tree tops. Pookie pookie." They were hysterical with laughter now as if they'd pulled off a million dollar heist, all except me, and Kiki, who looked disturbed.

Josh grabbed one arm and Lonnie my other as they carried me up the steps into the stinky cabin. It smelled like kerosene and nail polish. The kitchen wall was charred and the windows smoky. Gray drapes covered the windows except for one over the kitchen sink. It was dark like the minds of my captors. I screamed. "Leave me alone. Leave me alone. Let me out of here."

They pushed me down into a wooden chair and held me as Corey handed Josh a syringe. He shoved the needle into my left arm while Lonnie covered my mouth. I bit his hand and he whacked me across the head. "You bitch," he yelled at me and hit me again. Blurry eyed I watched as Kiki calmly received her dose and sighed with relief. They let me go. I whimpered until I felt the rush.

Oh my God, my head floated away from my body. I tried to fly. They watched me as I rose. I danced. I jumped. I felt light as a cotton cloud. I ran out the door into the light of late afternoon. The others followed. Kiki hugged me as if I were her best friend. "Don't you love it?" She laughed. "It's so sweet," and she danced with me. I wanted to live like that forever. I raced through the woods toward the lake. My insides burned as if I'd eaten a bowl of chili peppers. I loved it. I wanted to swim. I saw the lake ahead of me and threw off my blouse, didn't bother with my shorts, just plunged in and sank into that delicious liquid. I'd never felt like this. It was wonderful. I was wonderful. I could conquer the world. Lonnie took hold of me and tried to buss me, but I pushed him away. I wanted Kurt, but there was no Kurt around. Then Josh pulled me in. I heard Dorene squeal with delight. Josh was nude. I grabbed his balls and squeezed as hard as I could. He screeched like a rabbit in the clutches of an owl. Kiki put her arm around me and guided back to shore. I was crying now and laughing. I didn't know who I was. I'd forgotten that I was in danger, but it didn't seem to matter now.

Suddenly, I heard a loud voice from a bull horn, "This is the sheriff. You are all under arrest. Stand where you are with your hands in the air." Through my blurry eyes I saw a man come toward me that I recognized. It was Coleman. He said, "You're safe now." I didn't believe him. What did he want with me? I backed away and he stopped. "I'm here to help you," he affirmed. I didn't trust him.

Just then the cabin door opened and out leaped Josh, screaming, "You fucking Judas," and fired shots at Coleman, who dropped to the ground, blood pouring from his torso and head. More gun shots and Josh was down. My head was reeling. I saw blood everywhere. We were in a war. I screamed. Lonnie, still nude, ran to Josh swearing at the police who held the others at bay. The police swarmed around them while one checked the pulse of Josh, another used CPR on Coleman. "Put on your clothes. We're taking you in," Sheriff said to all.

Anderson emerged through the trees running toward me. I threw my arms around him. "Thank God, you're all right," he cried. He hugged me. I melted into his arms, into his safety. An officer brought a blanket to cover me and Anderson led me down the road to his car. I wanted to drive, but he said no. "You rest," he said, "Just relax, take deep breaths."

I did what he said and felt the air rush into my lungs. I loved the air. I wanted to breathe and breathe and breathe. I felt myself fading. That was all I remembered. When I awoke at the Anderson cabin, Mom was sitting beside me, rubbing the bruise on my arm where the needle went in. I couldn't make out what an officer was saying as he talked to my dad. My body felt like lead. I thought ropes were tied to my hands and feet holding me down. I hated this feeling. I'd fallen into a well. I couldn't swim. I was crying but I didn't know why. Bugs crawled up my arm but all I saw was Mom's hand rubbing. I pulled the blanket around me to stop the shivering. I wanted more of that gift Josh gave me. I felt like shit. I sat up and studied the room. I didn't know where I was. I hugged Mom.

The officer approached me, knelt beside me. "Thank God, you left a message for your Dad. If you hadn't, we may not have rescued you. Your kidnappers are in custody and will face severe penalties. Coleman was on to them, but your Dad's call sent us into action. We knew they were using but we didn't know where their lab was. Coleman found you via your cell phone in Lonnie Pepper's pants pocket. You need to be checked out at the clinic, a few tests to be sure you're all right."

I screamed. They shot him. I knew I was hallucinating but I couldn't stop. Blood covered me. I ran to the kitchen and washed my arms and face. I couldn't get the blood off. There was no blood, but I scrubbed harder. I stopped and turned to the officer. "Coleman was on our side?"

"Yes, he was an undercover agent."

"But he was having an affair with Dorene."

"No, he led them all on to get information. He was working for Bufords who suspected Richards fraud. He was onto Dorene and knew there were drugs involved but didn't know where they came from or what they were. Dorene hadn't heard the rumors about the two of them. She thought he was working for the Richards. Coleman had been following your investigation for some time."

I was too confused to know who I was or what I was investigating. I said nothing.

"How long have you been using Meth?"

"What's meth? All I know is that Josh stuck a needle in my arm and I floated away. God, it was good. I loved it, but it's gone now, down the well into the dark water. I'm drowning."

"So you've never used it before?"

"No, never. Oh, my God. Help me." Mom held me close. I was whimpering now, not crying, trying to find me in the water.

Dad was saying something I couldn't hear. Then he took my arm gently and helped me to the Prius.

The attendant in the ER looked into my eyes, took my temperature and had me swallow something. I felt like I'd fallen onto a feather bed. I wanted to sleep, but the officer was at my side asking questions. I answered the best I could. He wanted to know everything.

I told him about the plan Kiki and I had, but I couldn't remember what it was. I didn't know if I ever knew what it was and then the fear, the needle, mind flashing colors, the swim and Lonnie and then the blood. I looked into a war zone now as if I was a newscaster on the scene responding to a tv interview.

Coleman? How could I be so wrong about him? And Josh, both dead. This only happened in the movies, but I was there.

He said that I would have to testify and prove that I was not a user but a victim. I realized if Coleman and the police hadn't rescued me, I could have been raped or killed or both. I'd never forget their hideous laughter. I'd never forget my stupidity. Little pretty miss big britches. I didn't even know what meth was, but I knew its effects. "What's going to happen to them?"

"We'll, talk about that later," Officer Mason said. "You are released into your parents custody until you are asked to testify. For now get well. You'll be fine. The doctor reported no physical damage. You may need some straightening out in your head, however," and he smiled. "Step at a time."

He told me he had already talked with Kiki, who admitted that I was forced into the meth high by Josh who stuck the needle in my arm. She said that she tricked me into going to the Richards at the demand of Dorene who was acting on behalf of Josh and Lonnie. In other words it was because of Kiki and Anderson, who described what he saw when they rescued me, that convinced the authorities that I was an innocent victim of a plot. The two testified to both Lonnie and Corey nude and me in bra and shorts screaming, Josh blasting Coleman with a deer rifle and the pistol pops that brought Josh down. Because of them the police made no charges against me.

I WAS ALMOST myself again. We drove home, Mom, Dad, and I. The trees and roadways looked right again. They stood along the roadside waving slightly with the breeze, not dancing like fairy tale elves. A deer leaped across in front of us, so that Dad had to brake to avoid it, a close one. Mom reminded him the deer are out at dusk. It was dusk. She was shaking. It wasn't because of the deer. I slept.

When we arrived home after 9 p.m., Wendy was waiting for me in the driveway due to Mom's phone call. She threw her arms around me, fawned over me like a lost lamb brought back into the fold. We cried on each others' shoulders.

"I'm so glad you're ok," she blubbered. "Why didn't you tell me you were going up north with Kiki? I wouldn't have let you go."

"I don't know. I was a fool to trust Kiki, but she seemed to have changed. I thought she was our friend."

"I thought so, too, but I still wouldn't let you go."

"I know, but it's over now. Well, almost. I have to testify in Oneida County Court. Can you believe that Coleman was on our side?"

"No, I don't get it, either. We were so sure he was having sex with Dorene. How could we be so wrong?"

"Because he was a crafty spy, I guess. Kiki was the one who told us that. Now he is dead. Maybe not so crafty, after all, but I'd always be grateful to him for saving me."

"What about Kurt?"

"I've forgotten about him. Yes, What about Kurt?"

"He tried to tell me I was wrong about Coleman and that his relationship was only with Dorene. I think he loved her and knew she was in trouble."

"You think?"

"I don't think he was using. Maybe that's why he quit Dorene, because he couldn't save her."

"Then why didn't he turn her in?"

"I don't know. Maybe he knew the penalty if she was arrested and wanted to spare her."

"How is that sparing her?"

"Good question. I'm sure he'll be questioned."

Mom and Dad let us talk on the porch as we looked out through the screen into the stars that seemed close enough to touch, close enough to write songs about, close enough to include us in the universe. Wendy and I were together again, best friends, no more detectives, no more crazy adventures, just high school juniors working to prevent global warming and playing our instruments. I felt good now, content, knowing the ordeal was over. We could get on with our lives. Sort of.

PART THREE

Respite Along the Way

I WAS ON MY third session with a psychologist who had helped me return to myself. It hadn't been easy. In my nightmares I saw blood spurting from bodies, Josh, Coleman. The blood flowed all over me as I searched in vain for gunshot wounds. Once I attacked them all like superwoman charging, chopping, kicking, screaming at them to disappear. I, the heroine, ridded the world of devils, then I, the little girl, snuggled in her mother's arms who wiped the blood from my arms. I woke screaming until mother at my side held her little girl.

Each day mixed hope, challenge, confusion like an everything smoothie, made by my own hand that I made myself drink. Most of all I was thankful for life, for Mom and Dad and my brother John, who might have seemed like a bystander, but who cared for me and often counseled me through my trauma. He said I needed to focus on doing the things I loved. I did so because I knew he was right. I walked the rows of the vineyard, smelled the ripening grapes and watched the crows flash about overhead in the morning sun. That morning walk had become a ritual, a meditation, that allowed my senses to drink in air and the colors of the foliage all around me. The clarinet, too, drew me into its melodies, took me away into the wonder of the music that I made. I practiced hard, now with a goal to be first chair clarinet after fall auditions, and I succeeded. Our band director, Mr. Sullivan, a clarinetist himself and an excellent teacher, made it easy to practice. Wendy and I revived our woodwind quintet that was on hiatus during all the turmoil. Several questions haunted me, one of which was what to believe about Kurt. I couldn't wait to talk with him when he came home for Thanksgiving.

Long before my talk with Kurt, however, I thought about Tara Morissey. How distraught she had to be over the incarceration of her brother. I needed to talk to her. I wanted to understand how she and her brother could be so different. How was it that he had fallen so low and she unable to catch him? What about their parents?

I found her at her locker shortly after school began. She wanted me to come to her house to talk. She was not angry with me, but her cheeks were heavy like those of an old woman. She'd lost weight and hadn't tended to her hair or make up. When I arrived at her house on the southeast end of town, I discovered a disturbing scene. The open porch was in sad need of repair. The front door screen was torn and served no purpose. It flapped in the breeze. The leaves on the oaks and maples had yet to show their autumn colors. The lawn was brown, understandable because of the drought, but showed no sign of watering like the neighbor's grass next door. We sat in the kitchen across from each other at the aluminum edged table and fold up chairs. I had never thought of the Morissey family as being poor.

"Thanks for talking with me," I said, trying not to study the meager furnishings and unwashed dishes. Never had Tara given the impression that she lived in squalor. She'd always been clean and nicely dressed, not stylish, but nothing ragged.

She didn't say anything for a while, just looked at the table. "Would you like a glass of milk?" She asked.

"No thank you." I opened the conversation. "I'm trying to understand how your brother got into drugs, meth of all things, how he became part of that crowd. Did he ever tell you about what was going on with him?"

"Not really. I knew he was distressed. I've had all I can do to keep myself together. I understand why he needed a high. I've tried to get my high singing in the choir, but there's no choir in the summer. My father is drunk all the time or absent. Mom and I have had to bail him out of jail several times. Corey hates him. I don't hate him. He's like a child I have to take care of. Mom can't do it by herself."

I didn't tell her all I knew about his behavior with girls, even me. And I said nothing about his part in the beating of Hayward Russell for which no one was ever prosecuted. "I thought you and Corey were close."

"We used to be. We used to depend on each other, help each other pull through when dad was crazy drunk and I mean crazy drunk. I don't know where he is now. After Corey was arrested he yelled at us, 'You bitches. What kind of people are you? You don't know what your son and brother is doing?'

"To him Corey was no part of him, and I guess he wasn't and Corey felt it. Then he left. We haven't seen him since. We'll be better off. He won't take the money Mom makes at the cheese factory or what I make at Starbucks. But my school work comes first. I have to make something of myself. I won't live this kind of life forever."

I was stunned. I didn't know what to say, as you know that's quite unusual for me. I couldn't imagine living like that. She rose and walked to the door, clearly an invitation for me to leave. I followed and gave her a hug. "I want to be your friend," I said.

"Thank you. You are."

"Before I leave, can I ask you about Kiki?"

We sat on the front collapsing step.

"I've never known anyone so in need of affection," she said. "She has clung to Dorene like a parasite, drawing some kind of acceptance by doing what Dorene wants. She bought into the sexcapades completely and I think to live with herself she agreed to the drugs, first alcohol, then the meth. I feel as sorry for her as I do for Corey. I don't give a damn about Lonnie. What a shithead. He could corrupt an angel in a day."

"She had me fooled." I thought she had made a turnaround when she took up with Terry."

"She never spent time with Terry. He saw through her within a week or two of their courtship. She's a good actress, had starring roles in the school plays until she lost control of herself. My God what's happened to us."

"It's not the scene I imagined when we moved here. So much rotting wood under the veneer of propriety."

"You should be a writer."

"I am. I've joined the school newspaper student staff. I'm writing about this whole ordeal from the point of view of an investigator, a foolish, overconfident detective, who makes dumb choices. I'm taking my time to be sure I've sorted through all the facts and dispelled the fiction."

"If you include words about me and my family, will you show your work to me before you publish it?"

"Yes, to check for accuracy, but not to withhold information. If anything we've talked about today is off limits, tell me now."

She hesitated, then said, "No, as much as I wish what I've said isn't so, it's the truth and you can publish that."

I hugged her again and left.

Kiki haunted me the most. I couldn't believe she could deceive me so completely. When she spent time with Wendy and me, I was sure that she was honest about her affection for Terry and that she was trying to turn her life around. I didn't think much of her mood swings from time to time, because all of us girls went through a series of emotions almost daily. When Terry dropped her in the middle of our new found friendship, she said nothing about it. Rather she pretended their relationship was a nurturing one that gave her a positive outlook.

I had to talk to Terry before I went to the Buffalo county jail in Camden to see her. He, I discovered, worked as a layout designer for the school paper, so it wasn't difficult to find him. First, I had to gain his confidence and size him up. By now, however, I wasn't so sure I knew how to do that. I'd misread more than I'd read, apparently, but I needed to hear his story.

At that time the news room abutted the commons on the main floor in what one might call a large closet with one window facing outside and fluorescent lights illuminating the work area. Four stations with two Dell computers and two iMacs allowed us to brainstorm and edit our articles and commentary. Miss Jorgenson, a thirty something woman of medium height and auburn hair, was our advisor and teacher of the journalism classes, one of which I was taking then. Instead of study hall we journalists had permanent passes to this closet. Thank goodness it was air conditioned in spring and fall and heated in the winter. Both Terry and I preferred the Apple computers, so we often sat side by side. He had a wry sense of humor. When I asked him what he was writing, he thought for a moment and said, "Words, mostly Words."

"Do you put them in any particular order?" I teased.

"No, the computer does that when I shake it."

"I'll have to try that."

For the first few days of class and after the advisors introduction to the newspaper procedures, he questioned in a serious tone, "Are you going to write about what happened to you?"

"Yes, but I need some input from you."

"What input can I give you?"

"You were dating Kiki for a while. Tell me about her."

"What do you want to know?"

"I'm curious. She made it sound like you two were getting along famously, then she admitted on the way up to Riverton with me that she hadn't been seeing you for weeks. She said you curved and broke up."

"That's true. I found out she was using. She denied it, but it was obvious. You didn't notice?"

"No, innocent me, I didn't pay close enough attention."

"It was clear that her using was more important to her than me. So that was it. Too bad. She has a lot to offer."

"Why do you think she got hooked?"

"She craved Dorene's approval. She wanted to be a good time girl like her—popular, stylish, attractive, all the things she thought she lacked, none of which was true. She has much more to offer than Dorene, but she couldn't hear me. So I walked."

"What are you writing?" I asked.

"I don't know yet. I think it will be something about choices, how each choice determines one's destiny."

"Wow, heavy."

"Not really. The way I see it, all of us make harmful choices from time to time. That's the down side. The up side is that each day brings the opportunity for new choices. It's today that counts. Yesterday has an impact but it is not the determining factor. I also believe that to make good choices after bad ones one needs a mentor, someone who listens and guides and most of all cares. I wanted to be that mentor for Kiki, but she wouldn't let me."

"Maybe I can. Does she have a good relationship with her parents?"

"I think she does with her father. Unfortunately, her mother won't let her forget her bad choices and drags her down. I don't think it's intentional. It's just the way it is."

Once more I thought of my charmed life. What would my life be like without loving parents? I'd most likely be dead. They had always given me a long leash (forgive the dog metaphor) to explore but not so long that I got tangled in fences. Whenever I was lost, they found me.

I enjoyed working with Terry. I smiled at him without knowing it. Then I knew it and found it acceptable. I liked him. You notice that I made judgements based on meager evidence with words like 'like' or 'trust' or 'hate.' I had to do better at finding more nuanced words. Those words would come, I thought, with better judgement.

Next I had to visit Kiki. I wanted to thank her for her truthful account of what happened to me at the Richards. She more than Anderson testified to my innocence. I asked Dad for permission to visit her and he assented. The Buffalo County jail in Alma stands next to the county courthouse built from red bricks that had to be shipped in, probably down the river, at least 70 years ago. It looked like every county jail I had imagined, not that I'd imagined many. Sturdy iron bars on the windows keep people from crawling in for a nights sleep. Sorry, not funny. Actually the place gave me the creeps. I couldn't imagine living for days or months or years in one room with nothing more than a bed, a desk and a port-a-potty in the corner. I understood these quarters were temporary, but still…

When I stated my business, the officer in charge led me to Kiki's cell. (She was awaiting her trial.). The hall divides two rows of four iron bar cells with gray ceilings and floors. The place could have used a few flowers, something, anything to liven it up.

Kiki lay on her bed with eyes closed when the officer announced my presence. She awakened with a start and stared at me, wiping the blur from her eyes. Obviously, she didn't expect me to visit her. After all, I would be testifying in court about her indiscretions and her betrayal of me. I needed to know what was going on in her head, now that she was clean. I waited.

She looked at me as if I were her executioner come to take her to the gallows. I dared not smile or frown or make any gesture at all, just stood there facing her. I shouldn't have come. Did she fear me or hold me in contempt? Tense. I turned to go but she said, "Wait."

I turned back toward her and saw her Mona Lisa smile. "Sit with me," she said. I sat. "Why did you come?"

"I think to say I'm sorry, but I'm not sure what for. And I want to thank you for telling the truth about what happened to me at your expense."

"I'm sorry. You had to save yourself."

"Yes, but I couldn't save myself. I had to be rescued. Nobody can save herself, I've discovered."

She eyed me trying to understand. Suddenly she reverted to the lost soul that kidnapped me, "I'm going to the bucket, you know."

"Yes, but not forever." I thought of your role in what happened and before I could stop myself I blurted, "You almost got me whacked."

"No, I just gave you the high of your life."

"If you call me flipping and witnessing two killings, a high."

Then she flopped down in a fetal position. I sat beside her. "I hope you'll let me visit you."

She rolled onto her back and looked quizzically into my face. "Why do you want to?"

"Because we are friends." She heaved a tearful sigh and tried to speak, but instead she blubbered. "I'm so sorry, I'm so sorry."

"You know I have to testify. You know that, don't you?"

She struggled to comprehend. She'd have to think about that.

"I understand from one experience how easy it is to become a crack head. That high was bumping. I didn't want to come down, but I won't ever get cranked again. Never. Never," I said convincing myself. "I know that's not who I am or what life has to offer me and it's not who you are, either. You can rebuild. I know it. You can be who you are, not some phony carnival junkie on a perpetual roller coaster ride. That's not you."

She sat up and pulled me close. I hugged her back. "You'll make it," I whispered. She held on until the officer opened the cell door and said it was time to go. As I pulled away we smiled at each other.

"See you in court," I said.

"I understand," she smiled.

I thought she did.

I told Mom and Dad about my visit and he kissed me on the forehead that seemed a kind of anointing, maybe a commencement into a new world, a scary, delightful world of possibilities. "She's got to make it," I said.

"She will," Mom affirmed.

I thought about my misjudgment of Coleman and his awful death at the hands of a demented meth cook and crank head whose blood still seeped into the ground outside his cabin lab. If I hadn't gone there with Kiki they'd both be alive. I was glad Josh was dead. I knew I shouldn't be, but I saw him as evil. He helped cause the death of Tanner Mortenson swirling us around in the back of his pickup on a high. He and Lonnie, another baddie, suckered Dorene and Kiki into sex and meth and deserved what they got. But I wouldn't let bad thoughts occupy me. It wasn't about them anymore. It was about me. I had to let go of my hatred and think of Kiki. And Dorene? How much was she the perpetrator of this darkness that entered our school, our town, the lives of all of us? How would her naive parents cope with what she had become? They overlooked her indiscretions that escalated from antics to misdemeanors to felonies and death. Their lives had become a living hell. I had to find some charity within me toward them if not for her. For my sake I needed to talk with Dorene. I needed to understand.

Martha Hinton had completely withdrawn from society. I learned that Margaret Buford had helped her get counseling to cope with her daughter's arrest and pending trial. She had, apparently, gone mental. Earl Hinton, on the other hand, had been ranting and raving about the unjust accusations and arrest of his daughter, even going so far as to carry a sign in front of the County Courthouse. "Kangaroo Court" and "No Justice Here." He was livid. He stomped back and forth like a whole army of a one man protest.

On Labor Day Monday Buford Post and Camden community had an annual parade that covered about a mile. Citizens from both towns and from surrounding communities came to enjoy the parading of the our marching band, the cheerleaders, the football team lining up in team formation, snapping the ball and running a few yards to keep up with the other entries. Of course, the Camden fire trucks, three of them, turned on their sirens, and kids in fireman hats sprayed water from a garden hose into the crowd and everybody screamed with delight. Dad and Mom rented a convertible with a large sign that said, SUNBERG WINES COMING SOON! Wavy. The crowd applauded. Then a flatbed truck hosted a group in green and yellow cheeseheads reminding all of the Packers and exhibiting ODEGAARD CHEESE, followed by a truck pulling a houseboat and a CRUISE THE RIVER, HINTON BOATWORKS. The Hintons weren't on the boat. Nobody was. Sonny Macray drove the truck. Police on motorcycles zoomed around the entries thrilling the kids. They rented them just for this occasion because they never rode them on duty. The crowd swelled so that only the tall people and the little shorties could see as we passed the Amoco Station, Buford Realty, Starbucks and Lucy's.

The band always delighted its audience. Myra Hornsby, who couldn't play the clarinet worth shit anyway, bumped as our drum majorette and blew the whistle to start the intro drum beat to "National Emblem" march, a favorite and a difficult tonguing exercise for reed instruments. Trumpets can double tongue, not so easy on a clarinet. I didn't know anyone who could do it, not even our band director, but he had a fast tongue, so I blew tooa tooa tooa tummmtahhhhhhh, tooa tooa tooa tummmtahhhhhh, tatattatah tummmtahhhhh, tatatatah tummmtaaaahhhhhhh, taaaaahhhhhh, tum tum tum taaaaahhhhhh, tum tum tum taaahhhhh, taaaahhhh, tump. And the drums played the street cadence: tatarumptatum, tatarumptatum, tatarumptatarumptatrumptataaaahhhh and on and on to which the spectators clapped in rhythm. It was super sweet and well needed after what the town had been through, much to my doing.

On such an occasion the townspeople with all their differences came together to party with the same unity they demonstrated in supporting the high school sports teams. No one expected the football team to be as strong as last year without Kurt Buford and the three other seniors who had gone on to college, but a strong nucleus of juniors and seniors could produce a successful season. The spectators applauded as they paraded in their uniforms and made formations. They threw footballs to kids in the crowd and expected the kids to throw them back. One kid didn't, so chalk it up to an athletics department expense.

So how did people feel about me. I thought they believed I was a victim not a willing user, except for a few who had opposed my climate change initiatives from the beginning. To them I was a fake from the start. Most, however, were bigger than that. While the illegal lumbering indictments were still pending, most believed that the Buford Lumber and Mill Works would be exonerated from any wrong doing and the Buford family was clean, well not clean, exactly, but not criminal. The jury was still considering to what extent Kurt was involved. He had admitted to withholding information to protect his friends. Nobody knew how that would play out. He was still at UW, red-shirted and would play his sophomore year if he didn't go to guardhouse. I hoped he wouldn't. I'd misjudged him on several points of the wheel. Although he was a good athlete, he was no hero. Neither was I. I thought I was a legit detective but turned out to be a noob. I had a lot to learn.

Now to visit Dorene. She could be sentenced to three years in state prison, and three years of probation. Same with Corey Morissey. Lonnie, that asshole—I had to quit thinking that way—faced five years in state prison and a $10,000 fine. Served him right. He was as criminally involved as Josh Richards, who was dead. I felt bad for the Morisseys, especially Tara, who remained close to him in spite of what he had become.

Even though Dorene had always wanted to smear my lipstick, I felt something for her that ranged from hatred to sympathy. I couldn't explain the sympathy part. I intended to visit her if she'd let me. She wouldn't. So I had to chill. When I stopped for gas at the Amoco, Hinton wouldn't serve me. His attendant did. Today it was Sonny MaCray. He smiled at me and told me to go to the community center to see his photographs of the Labor Day parade. "You'll like them," he said. So I did. One photo was a close up of me playing the clarinet in my red and white uniform. It was his way of showing his approval of me for all to see. That was the way I saw it. Maybe others did to. No doubt he had been a solace to the Hintons, too. He had such a kind heart.

THE TRIALS, IN which I was a key witness, began the first week of December after the several weeks necessary for the plaintiffs' attorneys to put together their defense. The prosecution, also, needed what they hoped was an air tight case to convince the jury to convict. The indictments were different for each one of the lawbreakers and needed separate trials one after another that would span a significant length of time. I didn't know how many times I would have to testify. I had the counsel of a fine attorney, my psychologist, and, of course, my parents. My dad would also be called as a witness. Kurt, too, was on call for testimony. I talked with him before the first trial date.

When Kurt came home for Thanksgiving, he called me. I didn't expect him to, but he did and I was happy to talk to him. I was sure now that I hadn't given him a fair shake but I still didn't know if he was legit. This time when we met I'd listen carefully, knowing that, at least, some of the things he had told me were true. I needed to find out which ones.

He came to our house with my parents' permission. From the newspapers my parents knew that Kurt had been implicated in several of the accusations levied against the violators. They let me meet with him alone. He said that officers came to the Madison campus with a warrant and took him in for questioning at the

Dane county sheriff's office. The Madison TV station reported the event with the note that the investigation of this red-shirted quarterback was inconclusive, that more of the participants in the sordid affairs had to be questioned and that many of his revelations had to be corroborated. Now he was home, looking sheepish and ten points down. We sat in the den that Mom and Dad had agreed to vacate for the occasion but made it clear that they would be within earshot. I wasn't worried. I was mostly intrigued.

His first comment was, "I'm sorry."

I waited and when he didn't speak I said, "For what?"

I had a litany of reasons in mind, but I wanted to hear what he thought was most important.

"For deceiving you. If you let me, I'll try to explain not as a justification for my lack of action, but to be legit." No doubt, he had said these same words to his Dane County interrogators, but it seemed hard for him to tell me. "The positive side of things is that I knew Marvin Coleman was a private investigator. My father hired him to probe into the Richards affairs, because he thought Richards was bending the rules and didn't want our company to be caught up in it. We could employ other lumber distributors if we needed to make a change. He allowed me to work with Coleman in the investigation. We had made some progress when you interfered." He paused, then continued. "You must know that I cared a lot for Dorene more than she did for me and I used you to make her jealous. But I liked you then and I still think you're wavy in spite of the way you treated me. You are so different from Dorene who I thought I could save. She was dreadfully promiscuous which hurt me deeply. She seemed so emotionally scarred, but I saw her as a beautiful young woman with great potential. Yes, we made love many times. She called it fucking. I hated that, but I loved her and wanted her to love me.

"That was the first down side. The second was that I knew she was using. I didn't know what, but it changed her mood. She wanted me in, but I refused and tried to get her to quit. She tried and for a while I thought she had kicked it, but that Memorial weekend was the last straw. She took a sniff and off she went like a wild dog in heat. I threw her language back at her with a "Fuck you," and left. On the way home I thought about you. How innocent you are and I wanted to keep you that way. I wanted you to quit poking around. I was afraid for you. We were stylin last summer, weren't we? Until you leveled hundreds of accusations against me and believed nothing I said."

"Yes, but you came onto me with that swampy kiss."

"You fixed me for that. I heard you called the police, but I never heard from them."

"They were protecting their town hero, and didn't want to believe I was in danger. I called them off but they came anyway and I had to tell them what happened."

"That was the beginning of their suspicions even if they didn't keep a specific record."

"Do you want something to drink?" I asked trying to ease the gravity of the situation.

"No thank you." He was very formal in his demeanor and report as if he knew I was writing a book and now I am.

"So I was right. You were using me."

"Yes, and you were using me to get information about Coleman and Lonnie and Dorene and Corey and even to Russell's beating last fall. But I couldn't tell you what I knew. My friends were the culprits. I knew it but I couldn't get myself to talk. I thought maybe I could just pull away from them with a respectable, talented girl like you, but I couldn't make you believe I was legit. I know it's all over between us. I want the best for you and had I been there, I hope I would have had the courage to intercede."

"I'm beginning to believe you." I felt sorry for him. "What's your status at the University?"

"Pending while the investigation goes on. I'm hoping for a minor penalty for withholding information. I told the truth under oath."

I was speechless at this point, trying to digest his words, trying to decipher them, trying to sort out fact from fiction. I was still the detective but now for a very different reason. I was still attracted to him. He just said that it was all over between us and perhaps that was for best. Besides, as I told you, I was hanging out with Larry Rappaport, the trumpet player even though he didn't have Kurt's appeal.

I got up to usher him out. He kissed me on the cheek, a tender, caring kiss with no passion in it at all, a brotherly kiss. It was truly over. He told me as he stepped carefully along the icy sidewalk. "When I graduate in business and marketing, I'll be back to take over the family business. I believe our company will be acquitted of any wrong doing. Only Lonnie Pepper who worked for us has been indicted, but not for anything we did. You take care of yourself. And thank you."

"Thank you?"

"Yes, for bringing all this to a head. You have given me the balls to do what is right."

Hardly knowing what to say, I whispered, "You're welcome." I didn't know if he heard me. I didn't want him to. It sounded inane, like superior me, a moral snob when really I was just playing detective. Even Wendy early on told me I was playing a game I couldn't win. In a strange way I both won and lost. It would take me some years yet to learn which was which.

On Tuesday, December 6, the trial opened in Buffalo County with Kurt as the plaintiff indicted for withholding information and aiding and abetting criminal behavior. I had to testify. I was distraught over what I was not sure what I knew. His lawyer, Gregory McKellen of McKellen and Casey, was a hot shot from Milwaukee who had defended many accused of drug abuse. He put me on the stand as first witness. My lawyer, Jonathan Andresen from Eau Claire, sat beside me with my psychologist, Dr. Mavin Matson.

After the swear in, McKellen approached and asked me, "Were you having relations with Kurt Buford?"

"No," I said emphatically.

"You didn't have sex with him?"

"No."

"Tell me about your relationship."

"We went on several dates during the summer months."

"Would you say those dates were romantic in nature."

"Yes, but we didn't have sex."

"But you were attracted to him."

"Yes, but I didn't know if I could trust him."

"Why is that?"

My lawyer leaped up and objected, saying that the witness was not allowed to speculate. But the judge allowed the question.

"Because I knew he was involved with another girl."

"Who was that?"

"Dorene Hinton. He told me that at one time he was in love with her and was trying to save her."

"What did he mean by "save her?"

"He knew she was on drugs."

"Did you ever see Kurt take drugs?"

"No."

"How about drink alcohol?"

"No, I never saw him drink."

"You're sure."

"Objection. She's answered the question."

"Sustained."

"You went out with him even though you knew he was romantically involved with Miss Hinton."

"Yes, because he said he was through with her."

"But you still didn't trust him?"

"I don't know. I was drawn to him and wanted to believe him. He seemed truthful. But I wasn't sure."

"Did you see him at the Richards'?"

"No, but I heard he was there."

"Objection. Please strike what she said after, No. She can't testify to what she heard," Andresen emphasized.

"Sustained." The judge addressed me directly and said, "Do not testify to anything you haven't witnessed personally. Do you understand?"

"Yes, I'm sorry." I felt sick. I shouldn't have said that. I didn't know who had told me the truth and who had made up stories. Kiki, for example, made it clear that Kurt had sex with several girls, but Kurt denied it, so who was telling the truth?"

McKellen continued. "Did you see Kurt Buford participate in any illegal activity?"

"Objection. How is she supposed to know what is legal and illegal?"

"Sustained. Redirect your question."

"Did Kurt ever tell you that his father's company had dealings with the Richards?"

"Yes."

"Did he say what kind of dealings?"

"Yes, the purchase of lumber."

"Did he say anything about how Marvin Coleman was involved."

"He said that he was an undercover agent working for his father's company to investigate the Richards for illegal activity."

"Did he say for 'illegal activity?'"

"Something like that. That's what I understood. He said he didn't want Buford Lumber and Millworks to be involved in illegal lumbering practices and that he was working with Coleman."

"Did that surprise you?"

"Yes."

"Why?"

"Because of what I saw."

"And what was that?"

I tried to find a way out of the answer, because I knew now that I misinterpreted what I saw. My dad did, too. But I had to answer. "I saw him driving with Dorene Hinton as his passenger."

"And what did that mean to you."

"I know now that I misjudged the situation."

"My question is 'what did what you saw mean to you?'"

"I thought they were having an affair."

"And now you believe you have erred."

"Yes."

"Do you hate Kurt Buford?"

"No." I whimpered.

"Have you made up stories about him to get him in trouble?"

"No, I have not. I've just said what he told me."

"So you've broken faith with him, a man you care for."

"I suppose so." I was crying now.

"So it seems you've made a number of errors in judgement. You don't trust him to tell you the truth about his relationship with Miss Hinton, but you're sure that he knew she and his friends were using and didn't tell anybody about it. Am I right? You've made a number of misjudgments, haven't you?"

"Objection. If the defending attorney believes the witness has erred in judgement in any other matters regarding this case, let him be specific."

"Sustained. Mr. McKellen, you know better than that kind of question."

"I have no further questions."

"Mr. Potter, you may cross examine the witness." Mr. Andrew Potter, the prosecuting attorney, approached me slowly watching the floor as he walked as if the wood stripping would provide the answers to his first question, a question which to him was the crux of the matter, the answer to which could sentence Kurt to prison.

He raised his head and asked, "Did Kurt Buford tell you that he withheld evidence of criminal activity to protect his friends?"

He had me. I couldn't help but incriminate Kurt, but I had to tell the truth. "Yes, he did."

"Did he tell you what that evidence was?"

"He said that he knew Dorene was using drugs but he didn't know what kind."

"Anything else?"

"Not that I know for sure."

"But he may have known more."

"I don't know."

"I have no further questions."

"Mr. Andresen?"

"I have no questions, your honor."

"The witness may step down."

I felt like a dork. I told the truth, but I revealed what Kurt told me in confidence. He didn't say it was confidential, but that information could convict him. I might be the only one that he told. If so, I sold him out. I felt awful. I'd made too many costly mistakes. Was it a mistake to reveal what he told me? I had to tell the truth. If he had revealed what he knew to the authorities, two men might still be alive. I hated myself for getting me into this jam, for my stupidity, for the inflated opinion of me as self-appointed detective.

THE COURT RECESSED for the day. The next day Dorene testified in response to the prosecuting attorney's questions that she had sex with Kurt many times but that he never took drugs, that he tried to get her to stop, but she couldn't and didn't want to, so finally he left her. As far as she knew, he never had sex with anyone else. Kiki Bender was wrong about that. When asked when Kurt first knew she was taking drugs, she replied, "Sometime in March."

"So he knew for at least three months before the raid on the Richards that you and others were using," stated the prosecuting attorney.

"I suppose so."

"Yes or no."

"Yes," she hissed at him.

"So Mr. Buford broke the law by not revealing what he knew to the authorities."

"He wanted to protect me."

"And did he protect you? No further questions. The prosecution rests."

Mr. Potter had made his case and I had been his witness, emerged from the quagmire to convict Kurt. Damn me. Damn him. Damn the whole damn system.

Next up on the docket, Kiki Bender. I was first to be called as a witness. My lawyer and psychologist smiled as I was sworn in. I wanted so much to avoid any statements that made Kiki's legal predicament worse. I felt certain that in many ways she, like me, had been a victim. She was sucked into addiction and sex that she could find no way out of. I was on the verge of forgiving her for what she did to me. Maybe by suckering me into using, she could somehow justify her own addiction, a convoluted thought process I knew, but understandable to one addicted. I was ready to respond.

"The prosecutor, same guy, Potter, approached this time as congenial as he could be, smiling, and happy to see me.

"Good to see you again, Miss Sunberg. I hope you are well and rested."

I didn't respond.

"I have a few questions for you as I'm sure you know. Are you ready?"

"I guess so."

"Kiki Bender kidnapped you. Right?"

"Not exactly. I agreed to go with her. We had a plan to investigate the Richards Lumbering Company."

"And what was the plan exactly?"

"I really don't know. I trusted her. She seemed to know what she was doing."

"Apparently she did."

I didn't respond.

"When did you suspect that she had other plans for you?"

"When her mood changed after we made a stop and she used the restroom."

"How did she behave before and after?"

I described her change of mood.

"When did you become afraid?"

"I became more suspicious when she said she had a surprise for me. I didn't think the surprise would be a good one. But I wasn't really afraid until I saw Lonnie, Corey and Dorene. I knew then that Kiki was not on my side."

"Did Kiki take part in your abuse?"

"She watched and supported me during my high. She helped me out of the water with her arm around me. I remember that. We were kranked together. She seemed to participate with me. She laughed with me as if we were on a carnival ride."

"But she was the one who delivered you to your abusers."

"Yes, that's true, but she was a victim, too."

"I have no further questions."

Mr. McKellen, in her defense, asked me if I hated Kiki for what she had done to me.

"No," I said. "I feel sorry for her." Why did the attorneys wonder if I hate?

"You feel sorry for her, the one who delivered you into the hands of your abusers?" He was confident what my answer would be.

"Yes, I do. She's a good person. She told the truth when asked what happened to me even at her own expense. She wants out of this demeaning cycle."

"No grudges."

"She did endanger my life. I have to admit that."

"Do you want the jury to go easy on her."

"As easy as they can."

"No more questions."

The prosecutor called Kiki back to the stand and pinned her up against the legal wall, making her appear to be as guilty as the rest, but McKellen played the victim card, blaming her addiction and her entrapment by Dorene Hinton and Lonnie Pepper for her compliance. He made the jury seem like a choir he was conducting. He was bumping, much to my liking. Now we awaited the verdict.

Corey indicted for assisting in corrupting a minor, for manufacturing meth, and for using was facing up to five years in prison, but because he was only eighteen years old he would most likely get a reduced sentence. Both Kiki's and my testimony were on record so the prosecuting and defending attorneys referred to those accounts as foundation for their inquiries. He pleaded guilty to helping Josh Richards manufacture meth using three different methods and in participating in corrupting a minor. Now he too awaited sentencing.

Finally, the terrible twosome as I called them, Dorene Hinton and Lonnie Pepper took the stand one at a time. Once more I testified. When asked about Dorene's using, all I could say was that I saw her drinking, but I never saw her using drugs. Not that she didn't but I never saw her. I learned from Kiki, however, and I recounted the conversation she overheard, that she drove the get away car after Lonnie and Corey beat up Hayward Russell. The defending attorney objected to the testimony as hearsay and I suggested he call Kiki to the stand to confirm my testimony. Of course, the defense attorney would not do that, but the prosecutor did and Kiki confirmed my statements. At last, the culprits had been unmasked.

Then the prosecutor put Dorene on the stand and reminded her she was under oath and that false statements could lengthen her sentence. She admitted that she was part of the event.

"What was your reason for the assault?"

"Josh Richards ordered it."

"Why?"

"Because he was nosing around into their lumber company process."

"Is that the only reason?"

"He had been too close to the meth lab and needed to be jumped, you know, scared off."

"Some are saying that his death the next day from an aneurism was caused by that beating."

"You can't prove that."

"We probably could if we exhumed his body and did an autopsy."

"That's dark." Dorene scorned.

"Whether we do or not, you just testified that the meth lab was in operation as long ago as the fall of 2010, and you were a part of it."

McKellen was not ready for that nuance. His only defense now was to try once again to make her a victim of addiction. Clearly it didn't work. I could see in the faces of the jurors that they felt little sympathy for her. Potter had created a criminal threesome of Lonnie, Dorene, and the ringleader Josh, now deceased. The two remaining faced severe sentences.

The trial ended in mid-January, with a two week break for Christmas and New Years. The jury pronounced all guilty with recommendations for sentencing, Kiki the lightest and Lonnie the full book. Judge Martha Monroe announced her verdict to the anticipatory packed house of Buffalo county citizens. "Kiki Bender, I sentence you to one year in county custody and compulsory drug treatment, followed by one year of probation."

Kiki was in tears, tears of pain and of relief. It was a lighter sentence than expected. Dorene and Corey, on the other hand, were sentenced up to three years in state prison with drug treatment and counseling. Both showed the signs of addiction, the gray, loose-fitting skin, the weight loss. Dorene had lost the youthful beauty that attracted Kurt. Corey looked like an old man. Who knew what lasting effects would permeate his body and mind.

Lonnie Pepper, chief administrator to Josh Richards, known to the others as "the Cook," was his accomplice. For his accomplished distribution of the lethal drugs, for his beating of Hayward Russell, for the plot to kidnap and addict a minor to drug use, he was sentenced to 10 years with rehab counseling and psychological evaluation. The lumbering and toxic waste investigation continued under DNR watch and both state and federal agents in charge. The only verdict handed down so far was that the Bufords were exonerated. The focus was totally on the Richards and their partners in the industry. We waited for the verdict.

IN OUR HIGH school newspaper, *The Jacks Journal*, I published the story I'd been holding since the interview with William Buford the previous fall. At that time I had misgivings about his companies culpability. Since the exoneration, I could say all the nice things I had prepared with enthusiasm in honor of the generations of service the company and the family had contributed to the community.

The *The Camden Enterprise* picked it up and ran it in the community section without editing and with the comment that "the author, Libby Sunberg, is the teenage detective that probed into the Richards illegalities and discovered the meth ring. We look forward to her story that she has promised to write soon."

The newspaper had gained notoriety for its expert play by play coverage of the initial event and subsequent indictments, trials and verdicts. What it lacked was a personal account of the events that would have lasting implications.

Now that the drug part of the case was closed, Wendy and I returned to what I thought of as a normal life, but it wasn't. I didn't, for example, see Buford Post in the same way I used to. It was infected. Some of the sores had been treated, but others festered even if I couldn't see them. They were there somewhere, lurking. I hated that I knew that. I wanted the town to be as pristine as it was before all this happened.

Also, I wasn't the same person, the young woman that commanded attention with her presence. It was true that I had a jauntier walk, and a figure more womanly. But I was less sure of myself. My looks and my adventures were not really what this was about. It was much more than that. Those assets were, no doubt, responsible for initial connections. They led me to the discovery of dangers that I faced, to the edge on which I lived, how I could at any time fall into swirling water, how much I needed rescuing. Growing up is exciting and dangerous. Choices are risky. I like what Terry Adler said, that each day is an opportunity for new choices. While the past has its impact, we don't live there. Every day we re-create. Every place we go is a re-creation center and every person we meet is a re-creation. At least, that's what I was thinking at the moment.

I had to turn on the lights to scatter the darkness that hid in the shadow of trees. I'd noticed in the morning and evening that my shadow is much longer. Explain it as the earth turning or the sun rising and falling, but the truth is that at those times we are most vulnerable. In the morning it's what we are about to choose. In the evening it's what those choices have meant. Then the dreams mix the choices and the meaning like grape juice in a fermenting vat and in time produces a fragrant wine, at least that's what we hope.

I thought about those connections and my reactions to them. Handsome Kurt dazzled me with his swagger and romantic gestures, though I distrusted him. I liked Kiki from the start and still have an affection for her even after what she has done. Tara amazed me with her set of goals in spite of her home life. Wendy, of course, is still my best and most trusted friend. She and Billy Olson, who was a perfect lab partner, became very close. I was happy for them.

Dorene Hinton irritated me from the first moment. Not only was she a tyrant, she was also a slut. Sorry, I use that word because it's what she convinced Kiki to write on my locker door. I've tried to figure her out, but I've given up. She was cruel, controlling, dogmatic, promiscuous, unfaithful, conniving. She was despicable. I had the same feelings for Lonnie and for Josh.

The uncharitable part of me was happy Josh was dead. This world doesn't need people like him. Then there was Corey who I never cared for, never liked, but wanted him saved for Tara's sake. See what I mean? On the one hand I'm forgiving and charitable. On the other, I'm hateful and dismissive. Others will say I had reasons for despising those people. I suppose I did, but that anger ate at me. I should be happy that justice was done and let it go.

Then, too, I recognized how my feelings toward people were sometimes based on a cursory judgement, that proved to be wrong, but I held on to it like that judgment was the truth. I didn't understand me. My best qualities emerged through my energy, my commitment to problem solving, my willingness to take risks to do what was right, for my integrity, my love of the earth and of my family and friends. Those were the good things about me. I'm working on my downside.

The downside about me, I've decided, was that I thought I knew more than I did. That made me judge people falsely. It allowed for bad or good feelings to determine my behavior. Mom has said, "You can't help what you feel." I disagree. A person can change the way she feels about something or someone with more information and an open mind. Yes, I know I thought I knew more than I did. Sometimes I was quite wise, don't you think?

That brings me back to the vineyard I mentioned a some words ago. I love it. I think I've said so a number of times. The vines are pulling the nutrients from the soil, sucking up the water, absorbing the spring sunshine, and getting along with me just fine. We made it through the winter of my junior year, a relatively uneventful junior year. Since the sentencing of the players in the meth ring and the final verdict on the Richards' indictments, things seemed normal except for my wandering thoughts as I told you above.

Oh, I should tell you about the verdict rendered by an Oneida County judge whose name I've forgotten. What matters is that

Richards was held responsible for cutting trees on government property without a proper license. For that the company was required to replant not only in those areas but also on his own property. From now on the state DNR would determine where he could cut. The fine? $500,000. As for improper waste disposal, the company was responsible for clean up of the waterway and especially the toxic waste emitted from the meth lab that produced five pounds of toxic waste for every one pound of meth. Fine? $500,000. The judge demanded a tear down piece by piece of the meth cabin requiring the destructors to wear masks and carry the wastes to proper disposals. No burning was allowed to protect the environment. Then his company was charged with a share of the responsibility for toxic waste from the paper mill sewage and the smoke stack. The Richards portion amounted to $500,000. I thought Richards got off cheap. Still it was quite an expense to revamp the discharge systems and clean up land and water and tear down the cabin. I felt good about that.

To Hayward Russell I give thanks for initiating the procedure and for engaging us students in climate change concerns. Wendy was ecstatic to learn the outcome. I was too but less so because of the ordeal I had been through and the people involved whose lives had been so completely changed. While I was happy to have been part of the investigation, the trial and sentencing haunted me. I didn't know how prosecuting attorneys and judges live with themselves.

PART FOUR

New Vistas

S PRING WAS HERE and the Jr. Sr. Prom was just around the corner. Both Wendy and I were going, she upon the invitation of Billy Olson and I, with guess who. Right. Larry Rappaport. We were double dating. Wendy and I and Tara had been very involved in decorating to the theme, (My idea) "Let's Dance." From the internet we gathered photos of great dance scenes from the movies long past to the present: scenes from various Fred Astaire and Ginger Rogers films, Gene Kelly and Cyd Charise in *American in Paris*, Patrick Swayze and Jennifer Grey in *Dirty Dancing*, great dance numbers from *West Side Story*, *Singing in the Rain*, *Bye Bye Birdie*, *Footloose* and many more. We made panels of the posters and propped them up in the gym floor for the prom couples to dance around. Mona Thomas' mother, the dance instructor, would offer free instruction in ballroom dancing during the event. The drama department connected the multi-colored lights that would from time to time display crisscrossing rays from floor to ceiling and illuminate the faces of the dancers. The setting was magical.

On the second Saturday in May, the doors flew open to the music of the Savvy Pirates and singer Tiffy Tonisson from LaCrosse. She sounded like Taylor Swift, sort of. The emcee welcomed us all and thanked the parent and teacher chaperones for volunteering, pointed to the tables in white table clothes with name tags for all who signed to be in attendance and to the refreshment table of fruit punch and hor d'oeuvre sandwiches.

The four of us, Wendy, Billy, Larry and I found our table, close to the band and the boys stood in line to get the goodies. It was a happy occasion, one of relief and satisfaction. I was pleased to be with Larry, although our relationship wasn't legit romantic. We liked each other but I didn't think either of us believed it would last past high school. I didn't know what he was thinking. We'd never talked intimately.

Wendy, on the other hand, seemed completely devoted to Billy, and I think the way he looked at her, he felt the same about her.

After the dance we drove in Dad's Prius to Steward where we had reservations at Elma's Supper Club, a quality riverside restaurant with exceptional views of the full moon reflecting off the water on a clear spring night. No alcohol for us, of course, so we ordered sparkling apple cider to wet the palate in anticipation of the main meal. We had starved ourselves in preparation. Each of us ordered the salmon in caper sauce accompanied by green beans almandine and roast beets. We ate in silence, savoring every mouthful after a toast to Larry's upcoming graduation and acceptance to Lawrence College in Appleton. At the moment life couldn't be much better. Unlike some couples that carried on all night, we were home by midnight. We dropped Wendy and Billy off at his car at the school and I drove Larry home. He didn't have a car and wasn't interested in owning one. He biked where he needed to go. Good for him. He gave me a gentle, gentlemanly goodnight kiss. I didn't expect anything else. He wasn't the kind of man who would paw me as young men often tried to do, Kurt included, and that reminded me.

I haven't told you the outcome of Kurt's trial. He was mostly exonerated for wrong doing except withholding information, that the law determined was a misdemeanor in this case rather than a felony. He served no jail time, but had to perform several hours of community service and pay a $5000 fine, that his father lent him, I think. Maybe he gave him the cash. I don't know. The Madison Review reported the story of Kurt's exoneration and penalty and was pleased to announce his starting quarterback roll in the fall. He planned to stay in Madison for the summer to take summer school classes in business to lighten his load during football season. That was fine by me. It meant I wouldn't have to succumb to his invitations for romance if there were to be any. I know, he said it's over between us and I agreed. But I didn't know for sure. He still showed up in my dreams.

I should tell you, too, that as we were leaving Elma's, I recognized one of the guys who was at the houseboat party the past fall and pointed him out to Wendy who didn't recognize him. Whether he was involved in her nose twisting episode she didn't know. Obviously, we didn't ask him. That was over and done with.

I mention this because on Wednesday of the following week I was sure it was he I saw from my upstairs window under the willow tree in our back yard. He was looking up at me. I pulled the shade and calmed myself. Was I a target? Was he somehow connected to those indicted? Had he been sent to avenge his friends? What I had thought was over might not be.

I thought about the Hintons, if they were seeking revenge for my testimony against Dorene. They were visibly upset and Earl Hinton had never been friendly with our family. He was at issue with my climate change initiative from the start. Since the trial he'd never waited on us even though we always bought gas from him and would have had him service our Prius, if he worked on foreign cars. As you know he's a Ford man all the way. He was a single voice holding a placard denouncing the lack of justice in his daughter's sentencing. Maybe he was enlisting the Steward boys to do some dark and that dark might address me.

I told my parents about my suspicions. They couldn't quite believe that Hinton would put a couple of guys up to criminal assault. I say, not quite, because I could tell they were concerned. They offered no plan to deal with the possibility except to buy some bait and rent a boat from him for a short fishing excursion on the backwaters of the river. That would give us a chance to observe his reaction. It was important that he served us and that we show compassion for what he and his wife were experiencing. So that was what we did.

The following Saturday early about seven a.m. we parked in the Amoco parking lot and walked through the station to the bait shop. It was Memorial weekend, the anniversary of the event with Kiki Bender that began the sordid summer. Hinton was there. We thought he would be on a Saturday morning especially on this weekend when many tourists arrived looking for some Mississippi River boating and fishing. At first he didn't acknowledge our presence. "Good morning, Earl," my dad said as if they were old friends. "We'd like to buy some bait and rent a fishing boat."

"What are you fishing for?" He asked not looking up from the bait troughs.

"I think just sunnies and crappies."

"Make up your mind. That's two different baits."

"Ya, you're right."

"Crappies," I said.

I handed him my bucket and he dumped a scoop of crappie minnows into it without a word. My dad tried to break the tension.

"How's Martha doing?" he asked.

"How would you expect?" He snapped.

"Do you have a boat available?"

"How far you intend to motor?'

"Just the backwaters."

"I'll rent you a fourteen footer with a 15 horse Johnson. You can move fast enough and troll."

We paid him and followed him to the docks where he outfitted us with boat, motor, a pair of oars just in case, and life jackets. We brought our tackle box, casting rods, and minnow bucket.

"We're so sorry about what has happened," Dad said. "It has to be very difficult for you. We hope that she'll come through this and become the good person we know she is."

He just looked at Dad with such puzzlement like his assaulter who had knocked him to the turf and now offered his hand to help him up.

"I tried not to make it worse than it was," I explained. "I want her to do well." I didn't know if I meant it.

He trudged back to the bait shop without a "Good luck." We motored off to the backwater in search of crappies. Damn, no depth finder. We should have asked for one. Oh well, we had an approximate location in mind and found it after twenty minutes. A light breeze wafted the sun's warmth across the wavering reflection of the nearly still backwaters of the Mississippi on this perfect spring morning. No powerful current there, just a gentle nudge toward an island or sandbar, enough to engage the motor from time to time to right our course or return to a productive spot. We were father and daughter in this quiet place, undisturbed by other boats. A young man and woman passed by some distance from us in a canoe. I imagined what their lives were like, if they were in love, if married, if they struggled with themselves, but as they passed by I left my imagination with them. We caught a few nice crappies, Dad caught more than I, but then I wasn't really fishing. I smelled the mostly pleasant air except for an occasional whiff of a dead fish. Hinton had a cleaning house for us to use and offered us his knives to filet the fish. Dad was an expert.

He'd been catching fish in the Missouri River in South Dakota for years. Hinton smiled and said, "Nice catch."

I didn't expect to see the Sterling guy lurking around ever again and chalked it up to an over active imagination.

The next week Dad and Odegaard offered to display brochures of the attractions in Buford Post that included The Watering Hole, Lucy's, Starbucks, Buford Realty, and the Hinton Bait Shop and Boat Works. Kari Odegaard designed and arranged for printing free of charge.

At graduation Larry was handsome as ever in his red and white cap and gown. My family attended the ceremony and I joined his family at his graduation party that first Saturday in June. He managed to spend some time with me, but it was obvious he was looking to a future without me. That was okay, but I didn't expect it would be so obvious. I enjoyed so many of the friends we had in common including, of course, Wendy and Billy. That was the first time I'd been to his house, the first time I'd met his parents that were very cordial to me but clearly not welcoming me into the fold. His father was an attorney and his mother, a realtor for the Buford Realty. They had money. The party offered beer and wine for the adults and sparkling fruit punch for us. Fruit punch always seemed to be the offering for the young people. And the food—pizza, sandwiches, several kinds of ice cream in dry ice thermal containers, pastries, asian salads, enough to stuff us all many times over. After an hour or so of mingling and superficial conversation, I'd had enough. I wished Larry well, got a kiss on the cheek, said goodbye to Wendy and Billy, and departed.

I realized I was not driving home, just driving with the windows open to let in the warm late afternoon air, and to smell the lilacs that I love so much. I wasn't sure what my feelings were—contentment, yes to a degree, but also a melancholy, like an ending rather than a commencement. Larry and I had had fun together and now it was over. Maybe we both wanted more, but neither of us made it happen. I didn't know why I wasn't into him more, why in spite of all I admired about him I had no romantic inclination. For the moment as I drove I felt that sadness.

When I realized I was low on gas, I was in Sterling. I panicked. That might be enemy territory. I made a U-turn at the end of Main Street and headed home a little too fast apparently, because I the rear view mirror reflected the red light pulsing behind me. When I pulled over the patrolman asked to see my license. "You were doing fifty in a thirty-five mile zone," he said studying me.

"I'm sorry, officer, I'm kinda bummed out."

He recognized by my outfit that I'd been to an event that he assumed accurately was a graduation party. "Whose graduation?" He smiled.

I told him I was from Buford Post and that I'd just broken up with my boyfriend and was out on a drive. I buried my face in my hands and cried crocodile tears which worked. He said," I'm sorry, but you must watch your speed. You drive carefully." He let me go.

My false tears worked. I couldn't believe I put on that show for him. Somehow it lightened my spirits. I was ready for home.

ALL SUMMER I enjoyed my vineyard job. When not tending the plants and doing necessary maintenance, I read the books on the reading list for senior English and spent time with Wendy when she wasn't working at Swansons' Resort. We found time to practice oboe and clarinet duets and to gather for our woodwind quintet rehearsal. Unfortunately the French horn player graduated, so we looked for a replacement. Most important and life changing was that Grandma and Grandpa Sunbergs invited me to spend a week with them in Minneapolis to take a class of my choosing at their expense at the Loft. They knew I was writing for the school newspaper, so they thought I might enjoy taking a writing course. They wanted me to write my story. I wanted to, too, but not yet.

After the July 4th fireworks display put on by the city council at the Hinton Boat Works, Dad drove me to his parents in Southwest Minneapolis to stay for a week. I'd always enjoyed Grandma and Grandpa. They were easy to talk to and allowed me some leeway. Liz Merriweather, a Native American, who is an avid journal writer and blogger, taught the course. I liked her work. We met from 9 to 12 every morning for a week with a 15 minute break around 10 o'clock. Each day was a different approach. First day it was automatic writing on three starting words: river, dream and regret. I had no trouble with that exercise. The next day we started from a place where we loved to go or be. That was easy, too. One day it was on sadness; another on joy. We wrote for a half hour then shared with the other nine students in the class only if we wanted to. Fortunately, everyone was eager to share, except for the assignment on joy. I was surprised by the difficulty some, especially the three boys, had in writing about it. One girl was only in 8th grade but an excellent writer. The others were all senior high.

I particularly liked Jozy Nelson. She seemed so in touch with her emotions, so honest and descriptive. We always talked during our break. By Wednesday I asked Grandpa not to pick me up until 1:30 because Jozy and I were having lunch together by the river just three blocks north by Stone Arch Bridge, a lovely spot. We mused about our futures. She intended to attend the University of Minnesota after graduation from Southwest High School in Minneapolis and become a language arts teacher. She wrote poetry, some of which she read to me. It was very good, I thought, especially one she called "Rising from Water," that made me think about the Mississippi River passing over St. Anthony Falls, making its way past the locks down past my home in Buford Post and on. I've thought about that before as you know. She, too, read *Huckleberry Finn* the past year in American literature class and we dreamed about taking a house boat down the river, not really, but imaginatively. That was what I wrote about one afternoon.

I asked Grandpa about the University journalism school and he told me about the *Minnesota Daily* and the famous journalists that had trained there including Harry Reasoner, Erik Sevareid, and Roy Wilkins and more recently Garrison Keillor, Keith Ellison, and Jim Lileks. I began to have second thoughts about being a vintner back home in Buford Post. I loved the vineyard, the grapes, the aromas, and the maintenance work. That was all good, but I didn't think I could live my life doing it. Besides my brother had become the expert and a perpetual student. I think he had visited every winery within two hundred miles and studied every aspect of the process. He married the vineyard, so far not a woman.

After many delightful conversations with Grandma and Grandpa and as you would expect great salads and meals, I returned home.

I decide I had to discuss with Mom and Dad and my brother where my thoughts were leading me. One happy hour in early August I asked them to sit with me on the back porch and hear my thoughts. Dad popped the cork and John poured the wine while Mom extracted the always ready hor d' oeuvres from the refrigerator. I sat trying to be comfortable, not knowing what course my words would take. They sensed that what I was about to say had import and sat as if they were about to hear a eulogy. I didn't want it to be that way. When all were settled and somewhat comfortable I began.

"I've been doing a lot of thinking." I jumped right in, no introduction, no small talk, well maybe a little. "I'm so thankful that I've had this time with Grandma and Grandpa. We have such good conversations. They are really good listeners, too. I mused with them, let my mind go wherever it needed to and it needed to go a lot of places including the winery, Buford Post, Kurt Buford, my writing, especially my writing that, because of them and Grandma and Grandpa, I discovered more of myself. I reminded them of the detective in me and the need to tell the truth. Sorry, I'm just rambling.

"No, no, keep talking we're listening," Mom said leaning toward me.

"You know I love the winery, the whole business from beginning to end. I love the leaves and the aromas of the grapes pregnant with their juices that will become the Sunberg wines, but, and here's the thing… I don't see myself devoting my life to wine making, and I don't see my home as Buford Post."

"You HAVE been doing a lot of thinking," Dad said as he saw where this was going. "You mentioned Kurt Buford. What about him?"

"I don't know, Dad. He drops by in my thoughts every once in a while and when he does, it startles me. But, Dad, only our family holds me here, not Kurt. There may never be Kurt. Even though I love our home, the vineyard, the paths with the gazebos where people walk on a summer evening, I've never felt I belonged here. I'm not sure where I belong. Wendy and Billy are my only true friends, you know, but they will leave. Some really bad things happened to me here, but that doesn't make it a bad place, I know."

"Your mother and I have lived with your dangerous life. At times you've nearly scared us to death. But Buford Post is our home now in spite of its failings. We have friends and a very promising business. Also we can be part of changes that will evolve with our input."

"I know the Sunbergs will make this a better place. Will it hurt you terribly if I'm with you in spirit if not in person?"

Mother's eyes moistened. My words did sound like a eulogy. "Libby, we want for you what you want."

"I know you do, Mom, but I think you were hoping my future was here as part of the family business, but my time in Minneapolis has shown me a different life. I really want to be a journalist. For now my goal is to write for the *Minnesota Daily* and after that I'll see.

John, who had been listening carefully and observing the expressions of Mom and Dad, piped up. "I think this calls for a toast. "Libby, to you and your exciting future whatever it may be."

"Thank you, John. But you know you can't get rid of me. I'll be back whenever you need me to uncover some curious misdeeds." We laughed. The eulogy was over. There was more of the summer to enjoy and I made sure that Mom and Dad and John knew that I loved working in the vineyard and being part of this family. After all, I was not about to abandon Buford Post completely.

Occasionally Dad and I went fishing. Hinton had become more cordial. Dad asked about his wife.

"She's doing better. It's been very hard for her."

"And Dorene?" I asked.

"Martha and I visit her every week at the prison for women in Oshkosh. We don't think she's suffering any long term effects from the drug use, but time will tell. She sees a counselor regularly to work through some stuff. She comes home once a month for an overnight visit which is good for Martha, but I don't think it's good for her. She gets quite depressed when she's here. She won't talk to us about it."

That was the most Hinton had ever said to us, and that he spoke so honestly, made it a real break through.

"My wife hasn't forgiven you Sunberg's and especially you Libby for your testimony against her, but I realize Dorene was in real trouble and what you did might have saved her. Still it's very hard. I can't understand your politics, especially because you're a business man, Dan. Too much government. You've got to let business breathe."

"I know we have different opinions about how to do that, but I think you and I want the same things for our community and our families." Dad said no more. We were both happy that Hinton had been willing to talk.

"Tell you what, Earl. You post your Romney/Ryan signs all over your property and I'll post Obama/Biden signs, and let the best ticket win."

"Bullshit." He responded. "But you're okay, Sunberg. You got a good business going. It's good for the town."

"So are you going to get us some bait and boat and motor?"

"Yup. The large mouth will be in close to shore along the islands. Surface plugs are the best."

We climbed in the boat and motored out into the river feeling remarkably good and smiling. I didn't remember if we caught any fish. It didn't matter, not after that conversation with Hinton. Whenever we were fishing inclined, Hinton rented us a boat, offered advice about fishing locales, and seemed pleasant enough as long as we didn't bite on one of his argumentative statements. We were learning. Maybe he was, too. Wendy, Billy and I canvassed the neighborhoods to activate Democrats with some success. We planted the liberal signs.

The summer passed rapidly to the middle of August and the anniversary of my abduction. That's what I decided to call it. I was still traumatized by the memory and still aware of the high that meth induced. I was afraid of it. I always will be. I was afraid I could be a victim again. The next time by my own consent. I needed to stay away from bad company. Most of that company had dispersed since the scandalous arrests and convictions. The town had been in a stupor ever since, slowly recovering. The football and basketball teams hadn't been as strong without Kurt but still had a winning record. That helped. But every game reminded us of Kurt.

That fall, however, the townspeople would be able to watch him lead the Badgers football team on the Big Ten Channel and several locals including the Hintons had season tickets to home games. That was sweet. But you can see why I hadn't been able to process my feelings about this place. Furthermore I was not sure I wanted to live in the same town with Kurt Buford. I hadn't resolved my feelings about him.

Dad and Mom and John wanted me to apply to St. Olaf, John especially. He's an Ole all the way, but they understood my interest in the University of Minnesota. I applied to both before the winter deadline. My ACT scores qualified me for most of the best schools so I hoped for scholarships.

We were too busy in the fall for much entertainment. The grape yield had increased considerably and dad promised a stomping party, an idea that at one time was a laugh to Mom and now a brilliant idea. We sent out invitations to the surrounding area, advertising the first ten acres of the new Sunberg vineyard ready for picking beginning Labor Day weekend. "Volunteers needed to pick grapes and join in the grape stomp Sunday and Monday afternoon. Join the festive pig roast and squash meal for all comers and wine from last year's harvest." Mom printed the brochures with photos of the lushest grapes hanging from the vines and poured wines in the Sunberg Tasting Room. Dad and I distributed them all around chatting with people to come and bring their friends. We crossed our fingers.

That wasn't part of our mojo, but it worked. People came from everywhere. We passed out the grape forks for cutting and plastic bucket to put them in and off they went down the rows. We even hired a band to play "grape picking" music, whatever that was, and people swayed to the tunes as they picked bunches of grapes.

Imagine, if you will, a host of grape pickers eager for a taste of the remaining bottles of last year's wine and, we had to admit, the wines of other nearby wineries. We didn't have enough from last year's fermentation. That was our first big year and the larger community was happy to help us celebrate. The pig rotated on the the spit, the big batches of potato salad cooled in ice filled vats beside the chilled wines, and the cheeses from Odegaard's tantalized the volunteers' palates with bread from the Camden bakery. All was ready for the big event. Grapes filled three vats that waited for the first scrubbed down and hosed off feet to climb up the ladder and drop their bodies into the juicy mass with a Whee and an Aaahhh and a giggle. Each vat held ten to twelve people mostly in shorts, several young women in bikinis, a treat for the young men. I guessed word would get out and more stompers would appear for tomorrow's event. What one girl wore left almost nothing to imagination, but more eyes gazed on me in my short shorts and front tied blouse. One young man, I was embarrassed to say, revealed his interest too obviously, if you know what I mean. I kept my distance as much as I could.

You can't imagine what it's like to feel the grape juices between your toes and squirting up your calves with the sweet aromas of raspberries and blueberries and oranges and honey and lilac blossoms, so delicious, so wonderful. How exhilerating. This event put the Sunberg Winery on wine touring map. Smiles all around. Maybe I could be part of this business. Maybe my journalism career could bring me back here. But when I thought about it, I was uneasy.

Since Larry left for Lawrence College without any intent to keep our romance alive Travis Chapman replaced him as the first trumpet player. Also he figured he could replace him as my bae. Not a bad idea, I guessed. He was attractive, talented, funny, you might say quirky which I liked, and he had beautiful blue eyes to match mine. But he was not the only one thinking to replace Larry. Several others made themselves known as a possible suitor. I could have my pick. On the one hand that was stimulating; on the other, annoying. I didn't have good feelings about dating right then. I didn't want a hookup. I wasn't ready for that. Then, too, it wasn't that the field was so limited that I needed to make a selection. That was the blessing of beauty. I've made clear the curse of it. So I wasn't eager to get involved. Besides I had too much to do. Still I decided on Travis, just because. He was in band, he was cute, and convenient. Fickle me.

The first time Mom talked to me about my urges was last summer when she knew I was enamored with Kurt. It was a good discussion, not a lecture, certainly a concern. I admitted my attraction but also my anxieties about him, particularly his involvement with Dorene Hinton. I had no intention of having sex with him. She seemed somewhat relieved as she reminded me about safe sex. I didn't know if I should be offended or thankful.

It came up again when I was dating Larry Rappaport and I told her we were good friends, not passionate. "Don't worry," I said, to which she responded, "I can worry if I want to." That was Mom.

Mom and I discussed the topic again when I showed an interest in Travis. She liked him. I liked him. He made his presence known. Dad had only seen him from afar in the audience of a band concert, but had no objections. So we hung out together, Travis and I, often with Wendy and Billy. It was never Bill, by the way. Why was that? He was as tall and robust as any senior in high school. I thought I'd call him William to see what the reaction was. I encouraged Wendy to do the same.

"Good morning, William," I said to Billy in English class.

"Who?" He responded and looked around for someone by that name.

"You," I smiled.

"Oh, you mean William Theodore Olson of the law firm, Olson, Olson and Olson?"

"Yes, that's the one," Wendy remarked. "How does it sound?"

"What's wrong with Billy?"

"How about Bill?"

"I like Billy. It feels more like me with friends. Billy and Wendy, not Bill and Wend."

We laughed. Billy it was and all through their lives together. More about that later. He is such a dear.

Bottom line was that I took Mom's advice and started taking birth control to help me regulate my monthly cycle, at least that was what we agreed was the reason, not that I've had a problem. I did have urges, however, so far only when thinking about Kurt, but that hadn't happened for a while.

Thanksgiving came and went with the usual ecumenical church service, this time at the Catholic Church followed by family gatherings. Then Christmas blessed with fluffy snowflakes and lights all over town. We strung multi-colored lights along the eaves of our house and winery and let them twinkle for a few hours every night for two weeks. On Monday, January 2, Buford Post thronged The Watering Hole for the Rose Bowl game of Oregon Ducks vs. our Wisconsin Badgers which much to our chagrin ended in a loss of 38 to 45, an offensive shootout, well played and heart breaking. People mumbled on the way out offering advice to our coaching staff how to win a game and others content with a good, hard fought exhibition. Some fans attempted to start an argument when "You Can't Win 'em all" met "Why the hell not?" And a face too close for comfort. No, I wasn't there. Dad told me about it and chuckled.

The following week Kiki was released from jail after undergoing extensive drug rehab and completing her high school course lessons on line. She would graduate a year behind, in my class. In spite of trying to include her in our friendships, Kiki had become quite shy and removed. I thought she was ashamed. I was sure the counselors had worked to build her self-esteem. Without it, she could revert. I knew she didn't want that. She and I talked.

"I'm so sorry for what I did to you," she said. She said the same thing when I visited her twice in Alma, and she said it again. "I've told you I forgive you," I said once more. "Please know that the past is over. You are yourself now."

"I don't know if I want to be me."

"Yes, you do."

"I don't know who I am."

"I'm not sure who I am either." I told her about my misgivings about living my life in Buford Post at the winery, getting a degree in viticulture, and my interest in journalism. She didn't know what she was going to do. Then she told me that the court had reduced her crime to a misdemeanor instead of a felony, so it would be stripped from the record and not affect future employment. "You helped," she said to me. "You made it clear that you agreed to go with me to the Richards and didn't believe that I knew what was going to happen. Why did you say that?"

"Because I thought I knew you and that you couldn't be part of such a plot."

"But I was."

"I know, but you weren't like the others involved. I knew that. You needed help and you got it."

"Yes."

Slowly Kiki became her fun loving self, drug-free and productive. She'd be fine. I was sure of it.

I was accepted at both St. Olaf and the University of Minnesota, school of journalism on a scholarship that would really help. I chose the U of M. I wanted to write for the *Minnesota Daily* and become an investigative reporter. That was the detective in me. In July I spent another week with Grandma and Grandpa while I took the poetry course at the Loft. I got turned on to poetry in my American lit class my junior year. My journaling now was more poetic, I think. I tried to make magic with words.

What about Travis? He was becoming more passionate and I liked it. I knew it was going to happen and it did at his house in his room while his parents were in Madison for a class reunion. He wanted to talk about it, but I said, "No talk," and kissed him with my most luscious kiss and we melt together in a puddle on his bed. I started loosening my blouse, but he stopped me and whispered, "Let me." I let him undress me while I undressed him. He was magnificent. He said the same about me.

"I'm a virgin." I said anxiously.

"So am I."

"It can be messy."

He got a towel. We were both shaking, in anticipation, I suppose, and fear, maybe. Neither of us knew how to do this. It was supposed to come naturally. But it didn't seem natural, not to me. I wanted to be good at it and didn't know what to do to make it good. Then it happened quickly, painfully, and lovingly. Oh, my God. I was a woman with a man. I lay there beside him wondering what that meant. That was the most memorable moment of the summer of 2012. The rest of the summer I worked in the vineyard and volunteered to do weekly e-mailings and facebook entries for the Obama/Biden campaign. My romance with Travis ended when he went off to the Air Force Academy in Colorado Springs. We decided we couldn't maintain our relationship with each going in a different directions. Besides I still thought of Kurt even through all my doubts, angers, and misinterpretations that were both exhilarating and maddening.

THAT WAS ALREADY four years ago. So I'm in my final year in the School of Journalism and work as an apprentice investigative reporter for KSTP television in Minneapolis while continuing my work for the *Daily*. One of my assignments was to cover the

Trump campaign on April 2, 2016 in Eau Claire. Since Tara is in school there, finishing a degree in business, I arranged for her to have lunch with me. She was delighted. Sean Hofstedder, my photographer, and I drove his car to the site at Memorial High School where many had gathered to support the man they thought would "Make America Great Again." At the moment his candidacy lagged behind Ted Cruz by a few points, but he expected to get the Republican endorsement for President in July. I'm not going to tell you about the rally because you can read my report in the Minnesota Daily.

During the past three summers I spent Julys at the vineyard. Kurt returned from the U of W to Buford Post from time to time to see his friends and fish and, I suppose, to help his father at the mill works. We didn't see each other during his visits. Often I didn't know he had been here until after he had left. That didn't mean he was completely out of my mind. When he dropped in to our tasting room over July 4th week last summer, we had a good talk. Since then he has texted me several times to which I have responded. Our texting has developed into chats.

So with my consent Kurt came to visit me at the apartment that I was sharing with three girls in Dinky Town by the campus.

"I want to see you, too," I replied to Kurt's text. After a few more chats he made his appearance on a Friday afternoon in May, shortly before I graduated, and took me out to Vescios for a Italian dinner and a red wine, not one of ours, where we reminisced mostly, except for the news that he had enrolled in law school which, he said, would open the door to many opportunities. That meant he wouldn't be a lumberman. I was surprised. He said his younger brother would take over the business instead of him. I made it clear that "I'm a journalist. I can't be a vintner, even though I love the farm and the vines." As we talked, I imagined his kisses. I couldn't help it. I remembered. He mesmerizes me. At my suggestion we drove to a motel in Maplewood, a Comfort

Inn, and we made love the whole weekend. My heart nearly leaped out of my body."

So what does that mean for Kurt and me? I don't know. I know it takes more than love making to make a marriage. We'll see. After my graduation, a grand affair in Mariucci Hall, I was back at home finishing my story. Kurt is at the U of W working on his law degree. While I'm waiting to see if KSTP will hire me as a reporter, I'll be working feverishly to get Hillary Clinton elected. She should be a shoo in considering the competition. I'll keep my fingers crossed. It worked before.

POSTSCRIPT

'M SURE YOU want to know that Dorene is out of prison and working for her father at the Boat Works. Corey is out, too, working on a construction crew, I think. I don't know what Tara intends to do with her business degree. Wendy and I are in constant communication snapping and chatting. She is finishing her degree in music, specializing in oboe performance at Lawrence University and Billy is receiving his degree from U of W Eau Claire in biology with emphasis on Environmental studies. They see each other often.

Dad, Mom and still unmarried John, are enjoying their lives as vintners, planting more varieties of hybrid vines, especially the Marchal Foch for a delicious red and Lacrosse for an enticing white, as they learn more about how to protect these hybrids from the Wisconsin winter cold. I work the vineyard and serve wines in the ever popular Sunberg Mississippi tasting room. We've included the river name because it is as much a part of our lives as the growing town of Buford Post. It's here in Buford Post in these last three Julys that I have written my story so far. I get up with the sun, gaze out at the vineyard from the porch and write on my iPad. Early morning seems to be where past meets future, don't you think? No matter where my choices take me from now on, the vineyard and the river will live in me forever. Of course, I've sampled our wines. I really enjoy their bouquets and nuanced flavors and have become an amateur connoisseur.

I love to sit with my parents in the gazebo across the road with Wisconsin cheese and crackers and a glass of wine from our storeroom and watch the sunset over the Minnesota hills often in silence as we realize our blessings after all that has come to pass.

I should know soon if I have a job with a newspaper or KSTP. Whatever the case I believe I see up ahead another fork in the road.

By the way, Wendy Westin and William Theodore Olson are getting married August 20th. I'll be her maid of honor. Kurt will be there.

BOOK JACKET

N THE NOVEL, *A Fork in the Road,* Libby Sunberg tells her story that begins at the age of fifteen from a six year vantage point. During those years living in Buford Post, Wisconsin, where her family has a vineyard, she finds herself at odds with classmates who resent her liberal views and flirtatious manner. After her favorite teacher is beaten up on his doorstep and dies of an aneurism a day afterward, she, along with her new friend Wendy Westin begin their investigations that over the course of the narrative lead her into deep and dangerous trouble. She becomes the key witness in court testifying against several of her classmates that she also wants to befriend. Along the way she is drawn to the handsome school athlete who she distrusts as much as admires. Throughout her encounters she pines over both her genius and stupidity in a constant assessment of who she is and who she wants to become. The book is a tour de force coming of age novel that will keep you turning the pages and shaking your head in dismay and wonder.